Praise for the work of Ray Villareal

My Father, the Angel of Death is included in The New York Public Library's *Books for the Teen Age* 2007 and *Who's Buried in the Garden?* is the winner of LAUSD's Westchester Fiction Award.

"Villareal tells a taut and believable story about a young man's coming-of-age and the choices he must make. . . . Of special appeal to boy readers." —*Booklist* on *Body Slammed!*

"This wonderfully moving novel alternates between humor, tenderness and insight about what it means and takes to become a man." —*KLIATT* on *My Father, the Angel of Death*

"This story is written in a high-interest, low-reading-level style that makes it a perfect title for kids with reading-motivation issues . . . its appeal to its intended audience should be a smackdown." —*School Library Journal* on *My Father, the Angel of Death*

"Villareal takes on several important themes including illegal immigration, bullying, parent/teacher relationships and bilingualism. Ultimately, many of the characters—and readers—learn that there can be more than one truth, more than one point of view." —*School Library Journal* on *Alamo Wars*

"A solid glimpse at seventh-grade life from a writer who understands the age—biography reports, friendships made and lost, crushes, misbehavior and, sometimes quiet heroism. This story of three Latino boys with Stephen King-ish imaginations ought to find a wide audience." —*Kirkus Reviews* on *Who's Buried in the Garden?*

ON THE OTHER SIDE OF THE BRIDGE

OF THE

BRIDGE

Ray Villareal

PIÑATA BOOKS
ARTE PÚBLICO PRESS
HOUSTON, TEXAS

On the Other Side of the Bridge is made possible by grants from the City of Houston through the Houston Arts Alliance and the Texas Commission on the Arts. We are grateful for their support.

Piñata Books are full of surprises!

Arte Público Press
University of Houston
4902 Gulf Fwy, Bldg 19, Rm 100
Houston, Texas 77204-2004

Cover design by Mora Des!gn
Photograph by Jair Mora & Alexio

Villareal, Ray.
On the other side of the bridge / by Ray Villareal.
    p. cm.
Summary: Lon Chaney Rodriguez is a typical thirteen-year-old until his mother, a security guard, is shot and killed, and he becomes haunted by the feeling that he is letting her down by getting bad grades, skipping church, lying, and goofing off while worrying that he and his alcoholic, unemployed father will wind up homeless.
ISBN 978-1-55885-802-2 (alk. paper)
[1. Death—Fiction. 2. Conduct of life—Fiction. 3. Homeless persons—Fiction. 4. Hispanic Americans—Fiction.] I. Title.
PZ7.V718On 2014
[Fic]—dc23
                                                          2014022876
                                                                  CIP

Printed in the United States of America
October 2014–November 2014
Versa Press, Inc., East Peoria, IL
12 11 10 9 8 7 6 5 4 3 2 1

To my friend Ron Cowart, for his diligence and commitment to his work with the homeless population in Dallas, Texas.

"BE SAFE," Lonnie Rodríguez told his mother, as he always did each time she left for work.

He never worried about her, though. There was nothing really dangerous about working security at an apartment complex. Lonnie's mother was a basic rent-a-cop, who patrolled the area in a security car. She dealt mostly with noisy tenants, drunks, and kids riding their skateboards too fast in the parking lot. Anything more serious and she was instructed to call the Marsville Police Department to handle it. Lonnie's mother was armed, but she had never pulled her weapon on anyone.

When Lonnie was little, he used to make up stories about how his mother got into gun battles with drug dealers, thieves and murderers. Occasionally, she would drive the security patrol car home during her break, which added credibility to his stories. As far as his friends were concerned, that was a real cop car sitting in front of his house. It didn't matter that the emblem on the door said Wyndham Security.

Lonnie watched his mother drive off into the night, unaware that it was the last time he would see her alive.

CHAPTER ONE

"So you're telling me you didn't like *Feast of the Dead?*"
Lonnie asked. He flung a stone across the creek water's
surface and watched it skip four times before it sank with
a final plip.

"I didn't say I didn't like it," Axel said, balancing on a
seesaw he had constructed out of a wooden plank and a
large rock. "It's just that zombie flicks all have the same
basic plot. I mean, you always have a group of survivors
that spend the whole movie fighting off about a million
zombies. And in the end, it doesn't matter 'cause the survivors still die, or they get turned into zombies."

"People don't watch zombie movies for the plot,
Torres," Lonnie said, making a face. "They watch them
for the blood and the guts and the gore. And you've got
to admit, *Feast of the Dead* has tons of that." He skipped
another stone. "Boo-yah! That's seven!"

"Six," Axel said.

"You weren't even watching."

"I can watch and count and balance myself at the
same time."

"Well, it was seven," Lonnie said, though he wasn't
sure if he was correct.

"Whatever." Axel hopped off his makeshift seesaw
and joined him in skipping stones.

Lonnie tossed another one, careful not to get too close to the water's edge. The last time he went home with wet sneakers, his mother detected the foul odor and questioned him about why his shoes smelled like fish. Acting embarrassed, he told her that his shoes stunk because he hadn't changed his socks in three days. She chewed him out, saying that by the age of thirteen, he ought to know better than to wear the same dirty socks over and over. Then she made him put on a clean pair, which was fine with him. At least he didn't have to tell her the truth, that his sneakers smelled like fish because he had gotten them wet playing at Catfish Creek.

"Just one time," Axel said, "I'd like to see a zombie flick where they find a cure for zombie-ism, or whatever they call it, and people return to normal."

"That's never going to happen, Torres," Lonnie told him. "Don't you get it? Zombies are already dead. They're reanimated corpses. You can't cure the dead and have them lead normal lives again."

"Then what's the point of zombie movies?" Axel asked. "If there's never going to be any hope for zombies, if there's never going to be a solution to the zombie problem, then why bother making the same flick with the same ending?"

"Jeez, Torres," Lonnie said. "I didn't realize you were so sensitive about zombies. Maybe you should just stick to Disney movies."

Axel climbed on top of a boulder and stood on one foot, like a circus bear. "All I'm saying is that I'd like to see something original, a zombie flick that has some kind of hope."

Lonnie didn't know why he had bothered to lend Axel his *Feast of the Dead* DVD. He had missed the whole point of the movie. Zombies don't get cured. They don't get better. They multiply by creating other zombies until finally, they take over the world. That's what the zombie apocalypse is about. There isn't supposed to be an answer to the zombie problem.

Lonnie had seen *Feast of the Dead* with his dad when it first hit the theaters. Later, he bought the movie when it was released on DVD. He owned close to a hundred DVDs, a large number of them monster and sci-fi.

His dad, a horror film buff, had introduced him to dozens of horror movies, from the original *Nosferatu* and *Phantom of the Opera*, to the much creepier ones, like *Return to Darkness* and *The Butcher of Buffalo Bayou*. Over his wife's objections, he insisted on naming their son Lon Chaney, as a tribute to the legendary horror film actor.

Lonnie threw another stone, and this time it did skip seven times, but he didn't mention it. "Your family doing anything tomorrow for Labor Day?"

"I don't know. Why?"

"I thought we'd do something, maybe go to the paper company. The place will be closed, so we won't have to worry about the workers hassling us."

"I'll have to see," Axel said. "But like I've told you before, my mom doesn't like me hanging around you too much."

Lonnie looked up at him. "Why not? I'm always nice to her. I don't cuss in front of her or anything."

"I know. It's just that she thinks that your parents give you too much freedom. That they allow you to go and do whatever you want. She says you're a *vago*."

"A *vago*? What's that?"

"You know, a vagabond."

Lonnie sighed. "Okay, I give. What's a vagabond?"

Axel leaped off the boulder and landed next to him. "A vagabond's a drifter, a guy who wanders around from place to place, with nowhere to live."

"You mean like a homeless person? I'm not homeless. I've got a home, and I've got parents. Just 'cause I don't sit around the house all day like some momma's boy . . . "

Axel glared at him. "Are you calling me a momma's boy?"

"I didn't say you were a momma's boy."

"But that's what you're implying, right?"

"I'm not implying anything," Lonnie said, thinking how quickly Axel had switched their conversation from his mom criticizing him to his saying he was a momma's boy. "Look, if you want to get together tomorrow, call me. If not, I'll probably go to the paper company by myself."

Lonnie had never thought of Axel as a momma's boy, but he did feel that his parents were too protective of him. They hadn't allowed him to go to Regina Hulcy's birthday party at the Ice House because Axel didn't know how to skate, and his mom was afraid he would fall and hurt himself.

His parents also monitored everything he watched on TV. They would have gone ballistic if they learned that Axel had watched *Feast of the Dead*, plus a bunch of other horror DVDs Lonnie had let him borrow. Fortunately, Axel had a TV with a built-in DVD player in his room, and he watched the movies with the sound turned down.

If his parents thought watching horror movies on the sneak was bad, they would have freaked out if they discovered that their son sometimes hung out at Catfish Creek with Lonnie. But Lonnie had never forced him to go to the creek or anywhere else. Axel was old enough to make his own decisions. All Lonnie did was offer him an alternative to being stuck at home all day. It was Axel's choice to say yes or no.

Lonnie checked the time on his cell phone. Three minutes after twelve. "We'd better start heading back," he said and stooped to pick his Bible from the ground.

≈ ≈ ≈

The boys hiked up a hill until they reached the railroad tracks, which stretched above Catfish Creek. From up there, they could see the Winfield Road Presbyterian Church below. Service had just ended, and people were making their way toward the parking lot.

They ran down the hill, stopping at the bottom to pick grass burrs off their pants. They climbed over the fence behind the church, hurried inside the building through the rear door, and walked down the hallway until they reached the sanctuary. Then they slipped out the front doors, avoiding making eye contact with the Reverend Rodney Elrod, who was talking with a group of ladies about a women's retreat.

"Call me tomorrow," Lonnie said before crossing the street and heading home.

Lonnie's parents weren't church goers, but his mother thought it was important for him to get some religion. When Brother Elrod stopped by their house one day to invite them to attend Sunday services, Lonnie's mother explained that she worked a late shift and couldn't make it to church, but that she would send her son.

So each Sunday morning, she made Lonnie walk across the street to the Winfield Road Presbyterian

Church, even though they weren't Presbyterians. If pressed about their religion, Lonnie's mother might have replied that they were Catholic. But Lonnie hadn't been inside a Catholic church since he was baptized as a baby.

His dad didn't care if Lonnie went to church, but he wasn't going to fight his wife on the issue. Although he had been raised a Baptist, he wasn't sure if he believed in God, but like his wife, he thought it was good if their son did.

Lonnie hated going to church, especially to Sunday school. The pastor's daughter, Jo Marie Elrod, who attended Aaron Wyatt Middle School with him, was in his Sunday school class, and she always made him feel stupid because he wasn't nearly as knowledgeable about the Bible as she was.

Jo Marie howled with laughter when Lonnie once asked Mrs. Finley, the Sunday school teacher, if Jesus could technically be considered a zombie since He had been raised from the dead. Mrs. Finley told him that his question was inappropriate, if not blasphemous. Lonnie didn't know what blasphemous meant, but he wasn't trying to be funny or cause trouble. He thought he had asked a perfectly legitimate question. He had planned to ask the same thing about Lazarus, whom he learned had also returned from the dead. The following day, Jo Marie blabbed it all over school that Lonnie Rodríguez thought Jesus was a zombie.

Lonnie begged his mother not to make him go to church anymore, but she refused to listen. She would stand on the porch, watching, until she saw her son cross the street and walk through the church's front doors.

Then one Sunday morning, Lonnie left the sanctuary to go to the bathroom. He didn't really have to use it, but he had to do something to avoid falling asleep, while Brother Elrod droned on about the book of Habakkuk.

He strolled past the fellowship hall and the Sunday school classrooms until he reached the back of the building. Stopping there, he looked out the window. The back yard had a kiddy playground set enclosed by a chain-link fence. Beyond the fence, he could see the hill that led up to the railroad tracks.

Lonnie stepped outside, quietly shutting the door behind him. He was alone. The little kids were in children's church, and almost everyone else was sitting in the sanctuary, listening to Reverend "Snore-rod."

Walking around the playground equipment, he thought that if he was a little kid, he would have enjoyed playing in the fort and coming down the slide on his belly, or crawling through the plastic tunnels.

He turned his attention to the fence, and a wicked idea began to form in his mind. He looked around. No one was watching. Without giving it another thought, he hurried to the fence and scrambled over it.

Lonnie glimpsed back at the church, feeling like an inmate who had just made a prison break. He couldn't stop now. He raced up the hill until he reached the railroad tracks.

He took in his surroundings: cedar elm trees and red oaks that had begun to sprout leaves in the warm, April air; black-eyed Susans, bishop's weed and dandelions that blanketed the hilly terrain. The sun shone brightly, and the wind caressed his face. Feeling liberated, Lonnie inhaled deeply and smiled. Mrs. Finley might have found it inappropriate, if not blasphemous, but he turned his eyes skyward and exclaimed, "Thank you, Jesus!"

On the other side of the tracks, he could see Catfish Creek. He would have liked to have gone down there, but he didn't have much time. The service would be ending soon. Instead, he remained where he was, playing on the steel rails, until a couple of minutes past noon, when he headed back to the church.

From then on, Lonnie spent many Sunday mornings, either at the railroad tracks or at Catfish Creek. And if his mother happened to be standing on the porch when church let out, she would see her son, Bible tucked under his arm, smiling like a saint, walking out of the Winfield Road Presbyterian Church.

Axel was Catholic, and he attended Sunday mass regularly with his family. Once in a while, though, he would tell his parents that Lonnie had invited him to go to his church. That way he could join him on his excursions.

Sometimes Lonnie wondered if sneaking out of church to play at Catfish Creek was a sin. Would God punish him for doing it? If He did, Lonnie figured the punishment couldn't be any worse than having to endure listening to the Reverend Elrod's coma-inducing sermons or his daughter's self-righteous, flapping mouth.

CHAPTER TWO

LONNIE'S DAD WAS SITTING IN THE DEN watching a baseball game between the San Francisco Giants and the Chicago Cubs when Lonnie walked in. An open bag of Fritos lay on the coffee table, along with two empty beer cans. Lonnie's dad wore blue-plaid pajama bottoms and a black T-shirt with a picture of Ghostface from the *Scream* movies on the front. His face was peppered with five-day-old stubble, and his hair stood on end, as if he had poked a finger into an electric socket.

"Hi, buddy, how was church?" he asked.

Lonnie sat his Bible on the coffee table and plopped himself on the couch next to him. "Alright, I guess."

"What'd they preach about?"

"The usual stuff. You know, about God and Jesus."

"That's good." His dad turned back to the game, unaware that each Sunday he asked the same questions, and each Sunday Lonnie replied with the same superficial answers.

Lonnie grabbed the Fritos bag and pulled out a handful of chips. "Mom asleep?"

"Yeah. She went to bed as soon as you left. But she told me to tell you that there's leftover KFC in the fridge if you're hungry."

The Giants scored first, with a two-run homer. It was a good play, but Lonnie wasn't a Giants or Cubs fan. The game he was looking forward to watching was the one coming up later between the Texas Rangers, who were leading the American League West, and the Oakland A's, who trailed them by only two games.

At the commercial break, he went to the kitchen and took the KFC bucket out of the fridge. Three pieces of chicken were left. He grabbed a Coke can and carried it and the KFC bucket to his room.

Piles of clothes, empty soda cans, chips bags, comic books and other junk lay on the floor. Lonnie's mother had long given up trying to make him keep his room neat. All she asked was that his door remain shut, so she wouldn't have to see his mess each time she walked by. Lonnie couldn't understand what the big deal was. It wasn't as if the neighbors were suddenly going to pop in and want to see his room.

He made his way to his desk, which was cluttered with empty soda cans, books, pens and loose sheets of notebook paper. He picked up a book, *The Dumfrees Move In* by Violet Sparks, shoved everything else on the floor and sat his food and drink on top of the desk.

While he ate, he leafed through the book, which he was supposed to read for Progressive Reading, otherwise known as "reading for dummies." The class was made up of flunkies, low readers and students with "reading motivation" issues. Lonnie figured he fell into the third category because he hated to read. No, that wasn't quite true. He didn't dislike reading. He read all the time — horror magazines, comic books and graphic novels. He had even read Bram Stoker's *Dracula*. Some parts of *Dracula* were hard to understand, but Lonnie took his time with it and discovered he enjoyed the book as much as any vampire movie he had ever seen.

The most amazing thing he learned from reading the book was that a fellow Texan, a man named Quincey Morris, had helped kill Dracula. Lonnie had always been under the impression that it was Professor Von Helsing who had put an end to the Count's reign of terror. Even cooler was reading that old Quincey had stabbed Dracula in the heart with his Bowie knife. He only wished Bram Stoker had added Quincey Morris shouting, "Remember the Alamo!" before doing in the Count.

Lonnie's sixth-grade reading teacher, Mr. Dreyfus, had described him to his parents as a "reluctant reader." That label preceded Lonnie when he moved up to the seventh grade, and he was placed in Ms. Kowalski's Progressive Reading class. But reading wasn't a problem for him. It was that he hated to read dopey, baby books, like *The Dumfrees Move In*.

The story was about the Dumfree family, who had moved from Phoenix to Los Angeles, but their house wasn't ready for them to live in. So Mr. and Mrs. Dumfree, their daughter Sally, their son Rusty and their dog Elmo had to stay with their friends, the Robinsons, until their house was finished.

It was an easy read, and Lonnie should have zipped through it in no time. But he found the story so boring that each time he tried reading it, he zoned out after a few pages.

He shut the book and picked up the instructions sheet for his book project. He had already completed the first part, which was to design a new cover for *The Dumfrees Move In*. The original cover art showed the Dumfree family unloading their van, while Mr. and Mrs. Robinson stood on the porch, smiling. The picture Lonnie drew showed a red faced Mr. Robinson, arms flailing in the air, not smiling, but cussing, as he watched the Dumfrees sit their suitcases on the driveway. He figured that was how his dad would have reacted if a whole family and their dog had shown up at their door. The cuss words, encircled with a word balloon, were made up of pound signs, question marks, stars and exclamation points.

In addition to the drawing, Lonnie had to write a summary of the story that needed to include the exposition, the rising action, the climax, the falling action and the dénouement. He hadn't understood what those terms meant when he was in the sixth grade, and they still didn't make sense to him. He had also been given a list of twenty questions to answer about the story. One of them read: *Which character do you identify with the most? Why?*

Lonnie didn't feel like he identified with any of them. Definitely not the noodle-brain Mr. Dumfree, who didn't have sense enough to wait until his house was ready before moving his family to L.A. Or his ugly, red-headed kid, Rusty. Lonnie chuckled, thinking he probably identified most with Elmo, the dog. Wouldn't it be hilarious if that's what he wrote?

The character I identify with the most is Elmo the dog because dogs can't read, and I hate to read stupid books like *The Dumfrees Move In.*

He finished the rest of his chicken. Then he flopped on his bed with the book. Within minutes, he fell asleep.

Three hours later, he was awakened by a knock on his door. His dad stuck his head in and said, "Hey, buddy, your mom wants me to pick up a few groceries. Wanna go with me?"

"Yeah, sure." Lonnie jumped out of bed, happy to get out of having to work on his project.

Until eight months ago, his dad had worked as a truck driver for the Merriday Trucking Company. But he was fired after he was arrested for drunk driving, and his license was suspended. Since then, he had been without a job. His only source of income was the unemployment checks he received every two weeks, which didn't compare to what he had been earning as a trucker—a fact that his wife never let him forget. Only recently had his driving privileges been restored, but no trucking company was willing to hire him.

Dressing up had never been a priority for Lonnie's dad, which explained why it didn't bother him to go grocery shopping in his pajama bottoms, Ghostface T-shirt and flip-flops.

His wife had tried to get him to pay more attention to his appearance, but his typical response was, "Why? I don't need to impress nobody."

At the grocery store, he grabbed a shopping cart and looked over the list his wife had written for him. Then he wadded it up and shoved it in his pocket. "What do you wanna eat tonight, buddy?" he asked.

"I don't care. Anything's fine," Lonnie said.

His dad pushed the cart down the frozen foods section. "Let's get some taquitos," he said, pulling a box from the freezer. "And some chicken wings. Oh, and let's not forget to buy sodas. Go pick out your favorites."

Unlike Lonnie's mother, his dad didn't have any hard and fast rules about what they should eat. *If it tastes good and it fills you up, that's all that matters,* was his philosophy.

As Lonnie walked down the soft drinks section, a girl around nine years old raced by, pushing a shopping cart with another girl, about the same age, riding inside it. Lonnie scooted out of the way to avoid being run down by their cart as the girls sped by, squealing with laughter. When they rounded the corner, a voice shouted, "Hey!"

Lonnie hurried to the end of the aisle and saw a worker from the deli section holding the front of the cart. He was ordering the kid who was riding inside it to climb out. Behind the girls, a woman stormed toward them. Lonnie would've liked to have seen what happened next, but something more interesting caught his attention.

His fourth-grade teacher, Mr. Treviño, was standing in the produce section, holding a watermelon up to his ear and flicking it with his finger, the way Lonnie had seen his grandma Salinas do, to check for ripeness.

Lonnie had always found it weird to see teachers outside of school, whether at the mall, the movie theater or in this case, the Kroger grocery store. It had been three years since he had been in Mr. Treviño's class, so he wasn't sure if his teacher would remember him. Lonnie certainly hadn't forgotten him.

Mr. Treviño played the guitar, and every Friday afternoon, they would sing in his class. His teacher also found ways to incorporate the fine arts in the other subjects he taught. During their study of the Texas Revolution, Mr. Treviño showed his students how to make models of the Alamo using shoe boxes. When they read stories from Greek mythology, he helped them construct a seven-foot tall, paper-mache Cyclops, using a chicken-wire frame. The students learned how to make marionettes. Then they wrote plays and presented puppet shows to the kids in the lower grades. Mr. Treviño introduced his class to books like *Old Yeller, Charlie and the Chocolate Factory* and *The Lion, the Witch and the Wardrobe*, and he read to them almost daily. Lonnie thought that if his other teachers had been as much fun, he might have done better in school.

He was unsure about approaching him. What would he say to him after all this time? Mr. Treviño sat the watermelon in his shopping cart and started down an aisle.

"Mr. Treviño?" Lonnie called, rushing up to him. "Hi, remember me? I'm Lonnie Rodríguez. I used to be in your class."

The teacher stared at him for a second. "Lon Chaney? Of course I remember you. How could I forget that name? How are you?"

"Fine, sir."

"What grade are you in now? Seventh? Eighth?"

"Seventh."

"Making good grades, I hope?"

"Yes, sir," Lonnie lied.

"Great. Good to hear that."

Lonnie's dad came up the aisle, and seeing his son with a stranger, pushed his cart toward them. "Who are you talking to, buddy?"

"Dad, this is Mr. Treviño. He was my fourth-grade teacher."

Lonnie's dad had never attended parent conferences, so he didn't know Mr. Treviño, but he acted as if he did.

"Good to see you again, sir," he said, shaking his hand.

Lonnie felt suddenly embarrassed by his dad's shabby attire. By contrast, Mr. Treviño had on black dress slacks, a white, long-sleeved shirt and a red and gray tie, clothes Lonnie guessed he had worn to church.

"Lonnie sure has grown since he was in my class," Mr. Treviño said.

Lonnie's dad scratched his bristly chin. "Yeah, I was hoping he'd be a football player, like his old man. I used to play defensive tackle at Abilene High back in the day. 'Course, I didn't have this spare tire then," he added, patting his stomach. "Lonnie wants to play football, too, but his mom won't let him 'cause of his low grades. You know what they say, no pass, no play." He ruffled his son's hair. "Maybe next year. Right, buddy?"

Lonnie's face reddened. He had just told Mr. Treviño he was doing well in school. Why did his dad have to make him out to be a liar? Changing the subject, he asked his former teacher, "Are you still teaching fourth grade at Lamar?"

"Yep. Same school, same room."

"And are you still doing all those cool projects with your students?"

The teacher smiled. "Well, as a matter of fact, next week, we're going to start working on a play based on the book *Jumanji*, by Chris Van Allsburg. The kids will write the script and make the props. I've already contacted the director of the Marsville Children's Theater Center, and he's allowing us to borrow some of their costumes. We're planning to present the play during next month's PTA meeting."

With a forlorn feeling, Lonnie said, "I wish I was still in your class."

"Thank you, Lonnie," Mr. Treviño replied warmly. "That is probably the highest compliment a student can give a teacher."

Lonnie's dad peeked inside Mr. Treviño's shopping cart and noticed the watermelon, a bag of charcoal and a package of hamburger buns. "Looks like you're getting ready to have a cookout tonight before the game."

"What game?" Mr. Treviño asked.

Lonnie's dad blinked in surprise. "You're kidding me, right? The Rangers and the A's are playing tonight on ESPN."

"Sorry, I'm not much of a baseball fan," Mr. Treviño said. "But you're right about the cookout. My wife and I are having a few friends over for dinner."

"And none of them wanna watch the game?" Lonnie's dad asked, still in disbelief.

Mr. Treviño shrugged. "If anyone wants to, I can turn on the television for them, but . . . well, I'd better go before it gets too late. It's been really good seeing you again, Lonnie. And it's been a pleasure meeting you, Mr. Rodríguez."

After Mr. Treviño left, Lonnie's dad turned to his son and said, "That's kinda strange, don't you think? A normal-looking guy like him not liking baseball?"

Lonnie watched the best teacher he'd ever had disappear around a corner. "Dad, not everyone's a baseball fan."

He snorted. "I guess some people can't appreciate a good thing when they see it."

CHAPTER THREE

ON THE WAY HOME, Lonnie's dad exited Interstate 27 and drove down the ramp, slowing for the red light ahead. At the intersection, he spotted a familiar figure standing next to the underpass.

"Hey, buddy. Check it out," he said. "Moses is back."

Lonnie sat up and looked out the windshield, surprised to see the homeless man standing at his regular corner. Moses had become such a part of the landscape at the intersection of I-27 and Peyton Avenue near their house that Lonnie wondered what happened to him when he didn't see him there anymore. He asked his dad if he thought Moses had found a job. His dad suggested cynically that, more than likely, he was locked up in jail.

Moses sported a thick mane of gray hair and a long gray beard, which was why Lonnie's dad had nicknamed him after the biblical character. He wore a faded, over-sized Dallas Cowboys T-shirt and brown, loose-fitting pants. In one hand, he held a WILL WORK FOR FOOD sign, in the other, a Styrofoam cup.

With a slight nod, he stepped off the curb and approached their car.

Lonnie's dad grinned. "Watch this, buddy." He rolled down his window and stretched out a closed hand. With Moses holding his cup in anticipation, Lonnie's dad turned his fist, flashed him a thumbs up and said, "Go, Cowboys!"

Moses gave him a dirty look and walked away.

"Dad, you shouldn't have done that," Lonnie said nervously.

"C'mon, buddy. It was just a joke. Moses doesn't care. He gets it all the time. And usually a lot worse. Anyway, those people are nothing but a bunch of druggies and con artists, I've told you that."

From the side mirror, Lonnie watched Moses walk toward the car behind them. The driver rolled down his window and dropped a dollar bill into the cup. Moses bowed appreciatively, then moved on to the next vehicle.

The day was overcast, but the temperature still hovered at near a hundred degrees, normal weather for Marsville, Texas, in early September. If the heat bothered Moses, he didn't show it. He continued to smile and nod at the traffic, as if he was a Walmart greeter.

When the light turned green, Lonnie's dad made a left turn under the bridge, and they headed home. A few blocks from their house, it began to drizzle. By the time they pulled into the driveway, the rain was coming down hard.

This was the first rain they'd had in almost two months. The lack of rain, combined with the city's strict watering restrictions, had caused their lawn to turn from a deep green in the spring, to a dry, straw color. Lonnie didn't care if the grass was green or yellow. If anything, because of the drought they'd been experiencing, the grass was growing slowly, so he didn't have to mow the lawn as often.

They burst through the kitchen door, dripping wet, with plastic grocery bags clutched in their hands.

"Woo! It's pouring out there!" Lonnie's dad cried.

Lonnie's mother was sitting at the breakfast table reading the Sunday paper. She looked out the sliding glass door. "Yes, I know," she said glumly, wondering if the rain would end by the time she had to go to work.

"Hey, buddy, tell your mom who we just saw," Lonnie's dad said after they sat the grocery bags on top of the kitchen island.

Beaming with excitement, Lonnie said, "Remember Mr. Treviño, my fourth-grade teacher? We ran into him at the grocery store."

"No, not him. Tell her who we saw by the I-27 bridge."

"Oh." Lonnie felt his enthusiasm fade. "We saw the homeless guy Dad calls Moses."

Lonnie's dad leaned against the kitchen island with his mouth hanging open, like a dog about to receive a treat. "And tell her what I said to him."

Lonnie was hesitant, knowing his mother wouldn't find the prank nearly as hilarious as his dad did.

"Moses was wearing a Dallas Cowboys T-shirt, and Dad acted like he was going to give him some money," Lonnie told her. "But instead, he stuck his thumb out at him and said, 'Go, Cowboys.'"

His dad hee-hawed, as if Lonnie had just told the funniest joke in the world.

His mother rolled her eyes. "I'm sure the man really appreciated that, Richard."

"Like I was gonna give that moocher anything," Lonnie's dad said, his voice turning sour. "The problem with those people is that they don't wanna work. They'd rather stand on the streets begging for money."

She turned her head toward the sliding glass door and sighed, having heard this speech before. "Even in the rain, Richard?"

"Especially in the rain," he said, punctuating his sentence by slamming his hand on top of the kitchen island. "Those homeless love it when it rains. It's a big, cash-making opportunity for them. They know people will feel even sorrier for them if they see them standing out there, all pathetic-looking."

"At least they're bringing in money," his wife said under her breath.

"What's that supposed to mean?"

"Nothing." She folded the newspaper, then got up to inspect the grocery bags.

"Are you saying that I oughta be out there panhandling with Moses? Is that what you're telling me?"

"No, Richard. Let's drop it, okay?"

"Hey, I'm not a bum. I wanna work. I can't help it if nobody will hire me. I mean, even your boss won't give me a job."

She looked at him wearily. "I've told you, Richard. You can't work as a security guard unless you're trained and certified."

"Trained and certified. Big deal. All you do is drive around the apartment complex in a security car. How much training does it take to do that? Maybe you think I oughta enroll in the police academy just to learn how to—"

"Did you buy the ground beef?" she interrupted.

Lonnie's dad calmed down, and his face turned sheepish. "I didn't know you wanted me to buy ground beef."

"It was on the list, Richard. That, and a bottle of ketchup. I told you I was making meatloaf for dinner tonight."

"Ah, well, don't worry about that." He pulled out the box of taquitos from one of the plastic bags. "I bought plenty of stuff for me and Lonnie to eat."

His wife scowled at him. Then without saying another word, she put away the groceries. Lonnie's dad retreated to the den to watch TV, and Lonnie headed to his room, relieved that they hadn't gotten into another fight.

His parents met when they worked at a Mexican restaurant called Mateo's. At the time, his mother was taking basic courses at Lake West Community College, still undecided about her major. On the weekends, she waited tables at the restaurant. His dad had recently moved to Marsville from Abilene, Texas.

Lonnie's grandpa Rodríguez worked as the superintendent of buildings and grounds at Hardin-Simmons University in Abilene, and as an employee of the school, his children were eligible to attend the university, tuition-free. But Lonnie's dad had no interest in continuing his education and refused to take advantage of the opportunity. After a heated argument with his family over his decision, he left home to start a new life in Marsville.

In addition to working at Mateo's, Lonnie's dad played the guitar and sang lead in a Chicano rock band called Los Brujos. On occasion, the band performed in clubs and bars, as well as for weddings and *quinceañeras*.

One night, he invited Becky Salinas to a gig at a club called The Bright Star. According to her, that's when she fell in love with him. After that, she tried to accompany him whenever Los Brujos performed.

The band leader, Gilly Sandoval, converted his garage into a recording studio, and he helped the band record a demo CD, which he then sent to various recording companies.

Richard convinced his girlfriend that a recording contract was around the corner, and that Los Brujos were going to rock the Latino music world. It was also during that time that he proposed marriage to her. Believing their days of waiting tables would soon be over, she agreed to marry him.

Six years later, Lonnie's mother, having long dropped out of college, was still waiting tables at Mateo's. Los Brujos had broken up, and Lonnie's dad had just begun working at the Merriday Trucking Company. By then, Lonnie was four years old, and his parents were struggling to pay the bills.

Wanting to better her life, Lonnie's mother applied for a job with the Marsville Police Department. Her father was a retired cop, so she decided to follow his career path. Unfortunately, she didn't meet the MPD's physical requirements and was rejected. She applied with other departments in the area, but for one reason or another, each one turned her down.

Undaunted, she enrolled in a police academy program at Lake West Community, and upon graduation, received her TCLEOSE license, which certified her as a Texas peace officer. Even with her certification, she still couldn't get a job in law enforcement.

With every police department door seemingly shut, Lonnie's mother settled for a job with the Wyndham Security Company, and she was assigned to the Sherwood Forest Apartments, where she worked the night shift. Still, she never gave up hope of one day becoming a cop and had planned to reapply with the Marsville P.D. when she felt the time was right.

≈ ≈ ≈

At six-thirty, Lonnie and his dad sat in the den to watch the pre-game show, while a tray of taquitos heated in the oven.

Lonnie's mother walked out of her bedroom, dressed in her uniform: a white, short-sleeved shirt, black pants and a Wyndham Security badge. She opened the foyer closet, brought down her gun belt from the top shelf and strapped it around her waist.

Smelling the taquitos, she called out, "Richard, I don't want to see any dirty dishes in the sink when I come home from work."

Her husband didn't respond.

"Did you hear what I said?"

More silence.

She marched to the den and stood in front of the TV with her arms crossed. "Richard, are you listening to me?"

"Yeah, yeah, I heard you."

"I'm serious. I'm tired of coming home and seeing the house in a mess. As long as you're not working, the least you can do is help me keep it clean."

Lonnie's dad narrowed his eyes. "How am I supposed to clean the house and look for a job at same time?"

"Don't play dumb with me, Richard. You know what I mean."

"I'm trying to watch the game," he said, even though the game hadn't started yet.

His wife shook her head testily. She turned to Lonnie and asked, "How are you doing with your book project?"

"It's coming along."

"Lonnie, you can't keep bringing home low grades," she said, frustrated. "You barely passed last year and . . . "

"Mom, my book project's almost finished. I just need to answer a few more questions, and I'll be done."

"I hope so." She grabbed an umbrella from the utility room and started out the door. Lonnie rose from the couch and followed her outside. His mother lingered on the porch, staring at the rain. Finally, she opened her umbrella and hurried to her car.

"Be safe," Lonnie called out.

The rain didn't let up all evening. Thunder boomed and cracks of lightning lit up the sky. Lonnie thought about Mr. Treviño. He wouldn't be cooking burgers outside. He and his wife and their friends would probably be sitting around the dining table, laughing and joking, enjoying oven-baked burgers, not caring that the Rangers were playing in Oakland before a rowdy crowd.

He also thought about Moses, huddled under the bridge, trying to stay dry. Or, if it was true what his dad had said, maybe Moses was still standing at his corner, looking pitiful, but secretly relishing the rain because it would help him pick up more money.

Thinking back to Mr. Treviño's fourth-grade class, Lonnie recalled him asking, "What do you want to be when you grow up?"

Some kids answered, "I want to be a doctor. I want to be a lawyer. I want to be a police officer. I want to be a football player."

Lonnie told Mr. Treviño he wanted to be a horror film actor like his namesake, Lon Chaney.

It occurred to Lonnie that Moses had once been a fourth grader, too. He had sat in a classroom and had studied math, reading, history and science. He had played in the school yard with his friends. Room mothers had served him cookies and red punch during classroom parties. He had gone on field trips and had worked on book projects. Moses might have even participated in school stage productions, like Lonnie did, when he was in the third grade, and had danced in their school's Cinco de Mayo program.

Lonnie wondered what happened that caused Moses to end up homeless. Did he once have dreams of becoming a doctor, a lawyer, a football player, a police officer or an actor in monster movies? If so, when did his dreams die? At what point did he realize he wasn't going to be any of those things? When Moses was in the fourth grade, did his teacher ask him what he wanted to be when he grew up? If so, what did he answer?

Did he say: "Forty years from now I want to be standing at the corner of I-27 and Peyton Avenue, on a stormy September night, stripped of all my dignity, begging for spare change"?

CHAPTER FOUR

LONNIE DIDN'T GET OUT OF BED until nine-thirty. The ball game, which the Rangers won in overtime, 7 to 6, ended after eleven o'clock.

His mother was asleep, and his dad was spending Labor Day at Gilly Sandoval's house, jamming with Gilly, Joe Lara and Mario Hernández. Though Los Brujos no longer performed publicly, they still got together to jam on occasion and to reminisce about what might have been.

After a quick shower, Lonnie served himself a bowl of corn flakes and a glass of orange juice. He thumbed through the pages of *The Dumfrees Move In*, hoping he could gather enough information to fake a book report.

He still hadn't heard from Axel, but it was early. Maybe he'd call later. In the meantime, Lonnie got started trying to answer some of the questions for his project.

The first one read: *Who is the author of the book?*

No wonder Progressive Reading was known as "reading for dummies." What was so challenging about asking who the author was? Anybody could look at the book cover to find out. Even Mr. Treviño never asked such easy questions.

Lonnie jotted down: Violet Sparks.

Question #2: *Who are the main characters?*

He listed each one, including Elmo the dog. Ms. Kowalski might disagree, saying that Elmo couldn't be a main character since he didn't talk. If she did, Lonnie was prepared to answer that Elmo had a name and was treated like a member of the Dumfree family, so he was as much of a main character as everyone else.

Question #3: *Which character do you identify with the most? Why?*

Lonnie wrote: I identify with Mr. Robinson the most because he was caring and compassionate toward his friends, and that's how my parents have raised me to be, caring and compassionate. And as Jesus said, love one another as I have loved you.

He couldn't help but laugh at his ridiculous response. Yet, it was the kind of answer Ms. Kowalski would eat up. At least he hoped she would.

He wished Axel would call, so he could rescue him from this insanity. The book project was frying his brain. Lonnie needed to get out of the house before he went completely bonkers.

He looked up at the wall clock. It was eleven-forty. Rather than waiting any longer, he called Axel. The line went to automatic voice mail, which probably meant that his cell phone wasn't charged. Lonnie considered trying the house phone but decided to drop by instead.

When he arrived and rang the doorbell, he heard Axel's little sister Daisy shout from inside, "I'll get it!" Seconds later, she opened the door. A ring of spaghetti sauce circled her mouth.

"Hi, Daisy. Is Axel home?" Lonnie asked.

"Who is it, Daisy?" her mother called.

She turned around. "It's *el vago.*"

Lonnie felt his face grow hot. Was that his new name at the Torres household? *El vago?* Mrs. Torres walked up behind Daisy and greeted him with a withering smile.

He didn't smile back. Where did she get off calling him *el vago?* And worse, teaching her daughter to call him that, too?

Axel joined his mom and sister at the door. "Hey, Lonnie. I can't talk to you right now. We're eating."

"That's okay. I'll wait out here until you're done."

Axel looked at his mom. Her mouth tightened, and she crooked an eyebrow.

"Hold on a second," he said and shut the door.

Although their voices were muffled, Lonnie could still make out their conversation.

"You just saw each other yesterday."

"Yeah, but it was church, Ma. You can't talk in church."

"I can't believe that boy even goes to church."

"Lonnie's not a bad kid, Ma. Really. He's one of the few friends I have at school."

There was a pause. Then: *"I don't want you gone all day. Maybe his parents don't care what he does, but I'm not going to have you roaming the streets, like that* vago."

Axel opened the door. "I'll be out as soon as I'm done."

Lonnie sat on the porch swing and waited. The aroma of spaghetti hung in the air, causing his stomach to growl. The cornflakes had long gone through his system. Axel's mom could have invited him to join them for lunch, but she probably didn't want *el vago* leeching off them.

A few minutes later, Axel walked out. "Okay, I'm ready. What do you want to do?"

"Like I told you yesterday, I want to go the paper company," Lonnie said.

Axel gazed up at the sky. "Think we'll be able to find anything good? I mean, it rained pretty hard last night." "Let's check it out anyway."

The Martex Paper Company was a recycling center two miles from Lonnie's house. The side lots of the warehouse were filled with mountains of cardboard boxes, newspapers, office papers, paperback novels, magazines, as well as dozens of other paper products. In time, they would be bulldozed into a concrete pit, where they would be crunched up to form huge bales. Later, they would be shipped to a paper mill.

Lonnie liked to go the paper company to look for comic books. Most of the comics were duplicates or had pages missing, but he could generally find a few in good condition.

They crossed the street and walked past their school, which reminded Lonnie of his book project. "Do you know what a dee-now-ment is?" he asked Axel.

"How do you spell it?"

"D-e-n-o-u-e-m-e-n-t."

Axel laughed. "It's pronounced day-noo-moh."

Lonnie looked at him, confused.

"It's a French word," he explained.

"So what does it mean?"

"Is this for your reading class?"

"Yeah. I have to tell what the dee-now-ment is for a project I'm working on."

"Say it right, man," Axel said. "It's day-noo-moh."

Lonnie pronounced the word correctly.

"The dénouement is the resolution of a story," Axel said. "You know, how the story ends."

"Why don't they just call it the resolution?" Lonnie asked. "Or better yet, the ending?"

"I don't know. I guess teachers want to fancy up the words 'cause we're in middle school."

They passed by the Ice House skating rink and the post office. Both were closed. Down the street stood El Farolito, a Mexican bakery shop.

"You want to pick up some *pan dulce* to eat on the way?" Lonnie asked.

"Nah, I just ate. But you go ahead, if you want."

Lonnie was hungry, but he didn't want to buy Mexican sweet bread if Axel wasn't going to eat it with him. "Maybe on the way back," he said.

"So what book do you have to read for your project?" Axel asked.

"It's called *The Dumfrees Move In* by Violet Sparks."

Axel stopped and gaped at him. "Dude, that's a baby book!"

"Yeah, I know," Lonnie said dully.

"I read that book when I was like, in the third grade." Axel started to tease him about it, but he sensed Lonnie's mood, so he held back. "Is that the kind of stuff they give you in Progressive Reading?" he asked, now sounding serious.

"Well, school just started, and I think my teacher wants to give us something easy to read so we won't get discouraged and not read at all."

"I don't get it," Axel said. "What are you doing in Progressive Reading, anyway? You read way better than I do, and I'm in an advanced reading class."

"I don't know. I just can't seem to get my work done," Lonnie admitted. "And I doubt I'll have my project finished by tomorrow."

"What do you have to do?"

Lonnie told Axel about the story elements that needed to be included in his report, as well as the questions he had to answer.

"Look, all your teacher wants is for you to tell what happened at the beginning, the middle and at the end of the story, so you can show that you read the book," Axel said. Cracking a smile, he added, "And don't forget to include the dee-now-ment."

"What about the questions?" Lonnie asked, ignoring his dumb joke.

"Have you finished reading the book?"

Lonnie let out a sigh of frustration. "Torres, trying to get through that stupid book is harder than swimming in quicksand. I just can't keep my mind on it. It's so boring."

"Don't worry about it," Axel said. "I've read *The Dumfrees Move In*. Call me tonight, and I'll help you with the answers."

Lonnie appreciated Axel's offer, but he felt he was demeaning himself by accepting his help. There was no logical reason for him to be struggling with a third-grade level chapter book. Running into Mr. Treviño had reminded him that he was capable of making much better grades. When Lonnie was in his class, he made the A honor roll once and the B honor roll three times. And he had the ribbons and certificates to prove it.

It was after he left Mr. Treviño's class that his grades began to tank. In fifth grade, students were departmentalized, and Lonnie was assigned to Ms. Menchaca for reading, which made him feel apprehensive because he had heard kids say she was a lazy teacher. The rumors about her weren't far from the truth. Their reading consisted mainly of following along in their basal reader, while a voice on a CD read the text to them. When they weren't doing that, Ms. Menchaca handed out reading comprehension worksheets so her students could practice answering questions in preparation for the standardized reading test they would take at the end of the year. They didn't read chapter books, and she never read aloud to them. It wasn't long before Lonnie started bombing out, not only in her class, but in his others, too.

In sixth grade, he was placed in Mr. Dreyfus' class for reading. His lessons, much like Ms. Menchaca's, consisted primarily of a basal reader and reading worksheets.

Mr. Treviño used to have a bulletin board in his classroom with book covers stapled on it and a caption above that said: DISCOVER THE JOY OF READING! Lonnie's problem was that basal readers, reading worksheets and baby books didn't bring him any joy.

As they neared the paper company, Lonnie groaned. "Aw, man, look who's there."

Slurpee was yanking on the chain and padlock that held the wire gate shut, cursing and grunting, because he couldn't get the gate open.

Herman "Slurpee" Gilmore was in Lonnie's Progressive Reading class, and he easily fell into all three categories that qualified him to be there: he had flunked the seventh grade, he was a low reader and he definitely had "reading motivation" issues.

In class, Slurpee would rock back and forth in his desk, making heavy, snorting sounds, and Ms. Kowalski constantly had to tell him to be quiet.

Slurpee lived at 711 Laclede Street, so Axel nicknamed him "Slurpee" because of his 7-Eleven address. Before that, Lonnie used to call him Renfield, after the mental patient in *Dracula*, but a lot of kids didn't get the reference.

Slurpee hated his real name, so it didn't matter to him which nickname he was given. "I don't care what they call me, as long as they don't forget to call me for supper," he would joke.

Slurpee hadn't gone to the Martex Paper Company to find something to read. The piles of paper products included lots of porn magazines, Slurpee's favorite type of literature.

He looked up at the barbed wire that spiraled across the top of the tall fence, wondering if he could climb over it without getting cut.

"Hey, Slurpee!" Axel shouted. "You'll never get in there that way."

He turned around, not surprised to see Axel and Lonnie, because they had run into each other at the paper company before. Tugging at gate, Slurpee said, "They got the door locked."

"Yeah, they do that when they close the place," Axel said. "But we know another way to get in."

Lonnie wished Axel hadn't mentioned anything about their secret entrance. He was the one who had discovered it, and Axel should have left it up to him to decide if he wanted Slurpee to know where it was.

Slurpee wiped away streaks of sweat that had trickled from his bald head down to his pimply face. He turned to Lonnie and nudged his chin. "Wassup?"

Lonnie smiled awkwardly, then looked away. Slurpee reminded him of the creatures in the movie *Mutants from the Abyss* that had crawled from beneath the earth to attack innocent cavers. The creatures had pale skin, over-sized foreheads and little beady eyes, just like him.

The boys walked along the side of the fence until they found a section with a large tear that had been repaired with baling wire. A warehouse truck had backed into the fence, causing the damage.

Lonnie shot Axel a dirty look to let him know he didn't appreciate him letting Slurpee in on their secret. Then he unwound the wire and pulled back the chain-link fence, leaving an opening big enough for the three of them to squeeze through.

Once inside, they rummaged through the mass of paper products. But as Axel had suspected, even though the sun was out, everything was sopping wet.

"Maybe we can find some stuff inside the warehouse," Slurpee suggested.

"We can't go in there," Lonnie told him. "The place is locked."

Grinning shamelessly, Slurpee said, "The fence was locked, too, but we got in, didn't we? I'm gonna try the door."

When he left, Lonnie blasted Axel for letting Slurpee know about their private entrance.

"What was I supposed to do? It was either that or go home and come back later. And I can't do that. Remember? I told my mom I wouldn't be gone too long, so—"

Axel was interrupted by the sound of shattering glass.

Lonnie looked up and gasped. Slurpee had used a cinder block to smash the small window on the warehouse door.

"What are you doing, man?" he yelled, then peered about, wondering if anyone had seen him.

Slurpee didn't answer. Reaching through the window frame, he turned the inside knob and opened the door.

Lonnie's jaw dropped as he watched him disappear inside the warehouse. "Aw, man, that idiot's going to get us in big-time trouble!"

Axel's face lit up. "You know, I've never been inside the warehouse. Come on. Let's see what's in there."

Before Lonnie could protest, Axel ran toward the door steps. Lonnie whirled around again to see if anyone was watching before joining him.

The warehouse was dark, lit only by the sun's rays seeping from the skylights above. The air was stagnant and smelled of must and mold. Huge bales of paper were stacked in rows throughout the cavernous room. Although the building was hot, a chill crawled up Lonnie's arms. He imagined a murderous fiend lurking in the shadows, ready to pounce on them at any moment. From the corner of his eye, he spotted a rat, the size of a 'possum, dart between two bales of paper.

"Let's get out of here," he told Axel.

"Wait, I want to look around first," he said, marveling at his surroundings.

Slurpee climbed on top of a bale of paper and savagely tore at it, grunting and snorting. Then he stopped. A green button on a pole caught his attention. He jumped off the bale and pressed the button, turning on an electrical motor. The sounds of wheels and bearings reverberated as a conveyor belt rolled upward, coming to an end above a concrete pit.

Slurpee hopped on top of the conveyor belt with his arms outstretched. "Hey, look at me!" he shouted as he rode the conveyor belt. "I'm surfing." When he reached the top, he ran back down and rode it again. "Everybody's gone surfin'," he sang in a monotone voice, "surfin' U.S.A."

After the third time, he jumped off and ran to a forklift parked near the office. He sat in the cab and grabbed the steering wheel with both hands, like a little kid playing in a toy car. "Hey, y'all know how to turn this thing on?"

From having seen the men operate forklifts at the trucking company where his dad used to work, Lonnie knew Slurpee wasn't going anywhere without the ignition key.

Then, as if he'd read Lonnie's mind, Slurpee said, "I need a key to this." He swiveled his head in the direction of the office. "I bet they got it in there."

He climbed off the forklift and tried the office door, but it was locked. Not about to let that deter him, he grabbed a pair of pliers from a leather pouch on the forklift and used them to shatter the glass window on the door. Once inside, he ransacked the office, pulling drawers from the desk and the file cabinet, scattering sheets of paper and file folders on the floor, while he searched for the forklift key.

Lonnie knew he should have gotten out of the warehouse, even if it meant leaving Axel behind. But he was too mesmerized, watching Slurpee tear the office apart, to move from his spot.

The sound of a car door slamming shut snapped him out of his trance. Lonnie ran to the door and looked out. Instantly, his face turned pale.

The gate was open. A security guard had driven his patrol car into the parking lot and was headed toward the steps!

CHAPTER FIVE

LONNIE RECOGNIZED THE GUARD as Otis Barnaby, a sixty-seven-year-old retired cop who was now employed by the Wyndham Security Company. When Lonnie's mother first started working at the Sherwood Forest Apartments, Mr. Barnaby had been assigned as her mentor.

"Torres, a security guard's coming!" Lonnie cried.

Axel saw Mr. Barnaby's shadow in the doorway. "Slurpee, let's go, man! A guard's coming!"

"Wait, I haven't found the key to the forklift," Slurpee replied, unaware that Axel had said, "*A guard's coming!*"

Mr. Barnaby stood at the warehouse entrance. He rested a hand on his gun and held a flashlight in the other. He aimed a beam toward the office window and said, "Hey! I see you. Come out of there."

Slurpee spun around and froze.

Axel and Lonnie hid behind a bale of paper. Hearing their footsteps, Mr. Barnaby pointed his flashlight in their direction. He pulled his cell phone out of his pocket and called 911.

Axel's heart quickened. "I can't get arrested, Lonnie!" he cried. "I can't go to jail!"

"Put your hands up and step out where I can see you," Mr. Barnaby commanded them. He returned his flashlight to Slurpee. "You, too."

Lonnie's mind raced for possible options. The first one was to turn themselves in. Mr. Barnaby knew him, so there was a chance he wouldn't arrest them. But he would surely tell their parents. Then again, Mr. Barnaby had already called the cops, and Lonnie doubted they would be as lenient, not after the mess Slurpee had made.

Mr. Barnaby stood his ground, blocking the only exit, waiting for backup. As a veteran police officer, he wasn't going to approach them alone since he didn't know how many suspects he was dealing with. Still, if Lonnie could somehow get him away from the door, there was a chance they could escape.

Axel was shuddering and spilling tears. "What are we going to do, Lonnie? What are we going to do?"

Slurpee raised his hands in surrender and walked out of the office.

"The rest of you, do the same," Mr. Barnaby ordered.

Lonnie didn't care what happened to Slurpee. But even if he and Axel managed to get away, they would still be in trouble because Slurpee would tell Mr. Barnaby and the cops that they had been at the warehouse with him.

An idea came to him. He didn't know if it would work, but it was all he had. "Slurpee! The back door's open. Come on! Let's go! Let's go!"

Slurpee dropped his hands and bolted toward them.

Believing his suspects were about to flee, Mr. Barnaby left his post and cautiously approached their hiding spot.

While he looked for the rear exit, the boys rounded five bales of paper and ran out the front door, hoping a squad car wasn't pulling into the parking lot. Luckily, the cops hadn't arrived.

Lonnie's ruse didn't last long. Moments later, Mr. Barnaby flew out the door behind them. "The three of you, stop where you are!"

"He won't do anything," Lonnie told the guys, knowing that the Wyndham Security Company had strict rules about their guards drawing their weapons. Mr. Barnaby wouldn't shoot unless he felt his life was in imminent danger.

Lonnie pulled his polo shirt over his head so his face couldn't be seen. Axel did the same with his T-shirt, and they continued running.

Reaching the gate, Slurpee turned back, his face uncovered, and let out a sharp laugh. "You're too slow, fat boy! Run, run, as fast as you can. You can't catch me. I'm the Gingerbread Man!" Then he shot Mr. Barnaby the finger with both hands.

"Slurpee, the cops are going to show up any second!" Lonnie told him. "Let's get out of here!" Still holding his shirt over his head, he yanked him by the arm, and the three of them tore off down the street.

They didn't stop running until they reached the Smile Easy Dental Center, where they hid behind the building, in case the police happened to drive by.

"Man, that was freaking awesome!" Slurpee brayed out. "Did that fat tub of lard really think he could outrun us?"

"That wasn't funny," Lonnie told him. "You almost got us in huge trouble."

"Yeah, if we got caught, we could've gone to jail!" Axel agreed, wringing his hands.

"There's no way that old geezer was gonna catch us," Slurpee said. "My granny can move faster than him on her walker."

Lonnie slapped him on the arm. "Hey, don't talk that way about the guard. I know him. My mom and him are friends."

"They are?" Slurpee said, surprised. "Well, there you go. He wasn't gonna do nothing to us. We didn't have nothing to worry about."

"Are you kidding me?" Lonnie said. "You busted the windows and destroyed the office. You think he was going to ignore that?"

Axel stared at his hands. "What if the cops dust the place for fingerprints? They'll know we were in there. If I go to jail, my parents are going to kill me!"

"Quit your whining, man," Slurpee said. "You been watching too many cop shows. The Marsville P.D.'s way too busy to waste their time fingerprinting the place. Right, Lonnie?"

He asked him as if having a mother who was a security guard gave Lonnie insight as to what the police might do when investigating a break-in. But he had to say something to calm Axel down.

"Slurpee's right, Torres. The most the police will do is take down a report and file it."

Axel stopped whimpering and wiped away his tears. "Really?"

"Yeah, I'm pretty sure, especially if the guard tells the cops that it was kids who broke in." Lonnie didn't know if there was any truth to what he said, but at least it helped Axel regain his composure.

They waited by the side of the building for a few minutes. Finally, Slurpee said, "I'm gonna take off."

"Go ahead," Lonnie told him. "But I think me and Axel will stay here a little longer. Just be careful. If you see a cop car coming, hide in somebody's yard or something."

Lonnie and Axel watched Slurpee hurry out of the Smile Easy Dental Center parking lot. Ten minutes later, they left, too, keeping an eye out for the police as they walked.

They reached Axel's house safely, and Lonnie hung around for a while. Then he made his way home, thinking they were in the clear.

But he was wrong.

CHAPTER SIX

THE FOLLOWING MORNING, while Lonnie lay in bed, he heard the front door open and shut. Turning over on his side, he pulled back the curtain and saw his mother's car sitting in the driveway. She had just arrived home from work.

He heard her footsteps outside his door, then a knock. "Lonnie, are you up?"

"Yeah."

"Get yourself ready. I'll fix you breakfast."

Breakfast? That was the farthest thing from his mind. Lonnie was still trying to recover from the nightmare he'd had.

He dreamed he was back at the Martex warehouse, this time alone. The place was dark, except for a faint ray of light that shone from above. Tall bundles, casting ghostly shadows, surrounded him, and a strong odor of wet newspapers and mildew filled the air.

Out of the darkness, a deep, raspy voice called out, *"Put your hands up and stand where I can see you!"*

Lonnie poked his head from around a bale of paper and saw a Wyndham Security guard. His first thought was that it was Mr. Barnaby. But as he looked closer, he realized it wasn't him. It was someone—or something— inhuman. The guard wore a Wyndham Security uniform, but his face and arms were covered with rotting flesh and open sores, with yellowish pus oozing out. His teeth looked like corn nuts.

"*I see you, boy!*" the guard-thing bellowed, starting toward him with slow, but deliberate steps. "*You can't hide from me!*"

A wave of terror welled up inside Lonnie. He backed away, trying not to make any noise. Then he broke into a mad run through the bundles of paper, which now formed a labyrinth, with endless tunnels and pathways.

Behind him he could hear the *clop, clop, clop* of the guard-thing's shoes as it picked up its pace.

"*You're not gonna get away from me this time, boy!*"

Lonnie turned to the right and hit a dead end. Back the other way he ran, made another right, then a left. Again, he was trapped.

"*Run, run, as fast as you can. I'll still catch you. I'm the Security Guard Man!*" the guard-thing taunted. Then it let out a chilling laugh.

Lonnie clamped a hand over his mouth in time to stop a scream from escaping. Right and left he zigzagged, but again he hit a wall.

"*I'm gonna getcha, boy! I'm gonna getcha!*"

Right, right, left. No good, either.

Right, right . . .

"*Gotcha!*" A pair of rotting hands seized Lonnie by the throat, and he gurgled a strangled cry.

He woke up and reached for his neck. Nothing.

After his mother checked on him, Lonnie showered, got dressed and made his way to the kitchen. His mother had already set a glass of milk and a plate of Saturday pancakes on the table for him. The pancakes got their name because his mother used to cook pancakes only on

Saturday mornings. When she began making them on other days, Lonnie still called them Saturday pancakes.

His parents were seated at the breakfast table, having coffee. Lonnie picked up on their conversation and realized they were discussing the break-in at the Martex Paper Company.

"Serves them right," his dad said. "You know, they refused to hire me. The supervisor, what's his name? Milton something? He promised he'd get back with me, but he never did. Later I found out that he hired two other guys."

"*Mijo*, isn't there a student at your school the kids call Slurpee?" Lonnie's mother asked, almost causing Lonnie to choke on a chunk of pancake.

He swallowed a deep drink of milk to dislodge the food from his throat. Trying to remain calm, he shook his head slowly. "I . . . don't think so."

"Are you sure? Because it seems to me that I once heard you talking to someone on the phone about a boy called Slurpee who had been suspended for stabbing a student with a pencil."

"No, Mom, I, uh . . . I was probably talking to Axel about going to 7-Eleven to buy a Slurpee. I don't know anybody called Slurpee. But you're right. There's a kid at my school who got suspended for stabbing another kid with a pencil, but his name's Kirby, not Slurpee. Jeez, Mom, why would anybody be called Slurpee? That's a weird nickname, Slurpee." Lonnie stopped when he realized he was babbling. He took another drink of milk.

"Some kids broke into the Martex Paper Company warehouse yesterday," she said. "You know my friend, Otis Barnaby? He works security in the area, and he got a call that the burglar alarm had been tripped. So he drove out there and caught three boys tearing up the office, but they ran off. Anyway, Otis told me that one of the boys called another one Slurpee. This Slurpee kid was big, two hundred, two hundred ten pounds, with a shaved head. Are you sure you don't know anyone at your school who fits that description?"

"Mom, I don't know anybody called Slurpee," Lonnie insisted. "Honest. Maybe Mr. Barnaby heard wrong. The kid's name might've been Stevie or Sidney or Stanley."

"Lonnie's right, Becky," his dad said. "Otis is getting kinda old. His hearing probably ain't as sharp as it used to be."

She shrugged. "Oh, well. I just thought I might've stumbled over a clue that could help the police with their investigation."

The word *investigation* made the hairs on the back of Lonnie's neck prickle. He scarfed down the rest of his pancakes. Then he grabbed his backpack and kissed his mother goodbye.

Before he reached the door, she asked, "Did you finish your book project?"

His book project! He had forgotten all about it. "Uh, yeah, it's ready," he lied. "I did it yesterday as soon as I got back from Axel's."

At the beginning of the school year, Lonnie had promised his mother he was going to try to bring up his grades, and at the time, he meant it. Once classes started, he slipped back into old habits.

He thought about when he could finish his project. Progressive Reading wasn't until fourth period, so maybe he could work on it during lunch. Since he and Axel shared the same lunch period, maybe Axel could help him with it.

≈   ≈   ≈

The moment Lonnie arrived at school, Bobby Arbuthnot and Noe Macías rushed up to him, grinning like a couple of jack-o'-lanterns.

"Hey, Lonnie! Slurpee told us that you and him and Axel broke into the paper company yesterday," Noe said excitedly. "Is that true?"

"And is it true that y'all almost got shot by a security guard?" Bobby asked.

"What?"

"That's what Slurpee's telling everybody," Bobby said. "That y'all broke into the Martex warehouse, and while y'all were in there, a security guard shot at y'all."

"Nobody shot at us," Lonnie said.

"And did Slurpee really give the guard the double-bird?" Noe asked, giggling like a first grader.

Bobby laughed. "I could see Slurpee doing that. He ain't scared of nothing or nobody."

Of course he isn't scared, Lonnie thought. *Slurpee's too stupid to be scared.*

The bell sounded.

"Listen, guys. Do me a favor, would you?" Lonnie said as they headed toward the steps. "Don't say anything about this to anybody, okay?"

"It's kind of late for that," Bobby said. "The whole school already knows about it."

Lonnie didn't know about "the whole school." Usually the whole school means a handful of students. Except that in this case, he was probably mistaken.

While he was hanging his backpack in his locker, Jo Marie Elrod came up behind him and said, "I heard about what you and Axel and Herman did yesterday."

Lonnie couldn't believe that the story had gotten around so quickly, even Jo Marie knew about it. "What did we do?" he asked, acting as if he didn't know what she was talking about.

"You know what you did," she said. "But more important, God knows. Just like He knows about how you sneak out of church on Sunday mornings." Jo Marie pointed an accusing finger at him. "Don't try to deny it, Lonnie. I've seen you go out the back door of the church and then come back in at the end of the service. I don't know where you go, but pretending that you're in church when you're not, is a sin, and you're going to have to answer to the Lord for it."

Lonnie flashed her a snarky smile. "If I have to answer to the Lord, can I just send Him a text?"

"Don't mock the Lord, Lonnie Rodríguez," Jo Marie fumed. "Don't you dare mock the Lord. Ezekiel twenty-five, seventeen says, 'I will execute terrible vengeance against them to punish them for what they have done. And when I have inflicted my revenge, they will know that I am the Lord.'"

"Yeah, well, thanks for the Sunday school lesson, Jo Marie. But I've got to get to class or Mr. Arrington might execute terrible vengeance on me if I'm late."

Lonnie grabbed his books and strolled down the hallway. Jo Marie rattled off something else, but he didn't catch it.

Mr. Arrington stood at his door greeting his students. Inside his room, he kept a wooden box that looked like a pirate's treasure chest. But instead of treasure, the box was filled with costumes Mr. Arrington wore when he taught about certain periods in Texas history.

During the first week of school, he dressed up as a Spanish conquistador, while he shared the story of Francisco Vásquez de Coronado and of his search for the

Seven Cities of Cibola. On another occasion, he taught the class dressed as the French explorer, René-Robert LaSalle.

Yvette Sosa was in Texas history with Lonnie. He had known her since the third grade, when they were in Ms. Camacho's class together. They'd also had Mr. Treviño as their teacher. After fourth grade, Yvette moved to Austin, but she and her family returned to Marsville this year.

Back then, Lonnie had a crush on her, and he thought she liked him, too. But in elementary school, he was too embarrassed to admit that he was interested in girls, so he shied away whenever she tried to talk to him.

Now, Yvette was easily the hottest girl at Wyatt Middle School. Only this time, she was the one who avoided Lonnie. He couldn't blame her, really. Why would she bother to pay attention to him when she had so many guys hitting on her? Maybe he'd tell her he had seen Mr. Treviño. He figured she might enjoy hearing that bit of news.

Yvette was standing by the window chatting with Megan Patterson and Lisa Yarbrough. Lonnie waited nearby for an opening. When the girls noticed him, they stopped talking. Unfortunately, all he managed to say to Yvette was, "Hey, you'll never guess who I ran into at the grocery store the other day," when the bell rang, and everyone took their seats. Mr. Arrington entered the classroom, reached inside his costume box and pulled out a long, priest's robe and a wooden cross.

After class, Lonnie tried to catch up with Yvette, but she disappeared into a crowd of students before he could reach her.

He headed to Mrs. Ridley's for math, a class he absolutely hated. They had been studying how to multiply and divide fractions, something Lonnie still couldn't figure out how to do. As it was, he could barely multiply and divide whole numbers.

Next was science, with probably the oldest living teacher in the world, Mr. Malone, a frail man with a gaunt face and a bony body. The kids joked that Mr. Malone taught science with his identical twin brother, the life-size skeleton he kept in his room. Lonnie's mind drifted as Mr. Malone, in a quivery voice, rattled off something about ecosystems.

By lunchtime, Lonnie's brain felt like mush. After he bought his food, he looked around for a place to sit and noticed a bunch of kids huddled around Slurpee.

"It was freaking awesome!" he heard Slurpee tell the guys. "The guard pulls out his gun and fires at me. Bam! But I duck. Then I shoot back with both fingers. Pow! Pow!" Slurpee demonstrated how he did it, which made the guys burst with laughter.

José Castillo called Lonnie over. "Did the guard really shoot at you guys?"

Lonnie sat his tray down at their table and glowered at Slurpee. "Nobody shot at us," he said.

"The guard didn't shoot at them," Slurpee told the guys, holding onto his fantasy. "He shot at me. Lonnie and Axel had their heads covered up, so they couldn't hear or see nothing. But that bullet flew right by my ear."

Lonnie realized he used to tell crazy stories like that when he was little, but he was seven years old at the time, not fourteen.

Axel entered the cafeteria. When José saw him, he motioned for him to join them.

"Did the security guard at the paper company really shoot at you guys when you broke into the warehouse yesterday?" José asked. "'Cause that's what Slurpee's saying, but Lonnie says he didn't."

Axel's face grew chalky, and he stared at Lonnie, speechless.

"Herman's just messing with you," Lonnie said, referring to Slurpee by his real name. After what his mother had told him, he thought it would be best if they ditched the Slurpee nickname. "We went to the paper company to look for comic books and stuff, but a guard chased us out of there. That's all that happened." Lonnie gave Herman a dead-level stare, letting him know he wasn't going to back him up. "Let's go out in the hallway real quick," he told him and Axel. "I need to talk to you about something."

By calling them away, Lonnie was certain the guys at the table suspected there might be some truth to Herman's story, but he couldn't worry about it. Outside the cafeteria, he shared what his mother had said with them.

"From now on, you can't let anybody call you Slurpee," he told Herman. "And you can't tell anybody else about what happened at the warehouse."

"But everybody already knows," he said.

"Well, tell them you made it up. Tell them you were just kidding."

Axel groaned. "Man, I wish we'd never gone to the paper company. If the police find out we broke into the place, we could all end up with criminal records. I probably won't even get to go to college."

"Chill out, Torres," Lonnie said. "It's over, okay? As long as Slurpee . . . I mean, Herman stops talking about it, everybody will forget about it in a day or two."

They went back inside the cafeteria and ate their food. Before long, the bell rang, and it was time for fourth period.

On his way to Progressive Reading, Lonnie thought about what excuse he would give Ms. Kowalski for why he hadn't completed his book project. He considered turning in what he had done so far, but decided that if he showed her the silly book cover he had drawn, he might make things worse.

After school, he found his mother sitting in the kitchen alone, staring at the wall, her face somber. He dropped his backpack on a chair and greeted her with a kiss on the cheek.

"Lonnie, sit down," she said. "We need to talk about something very important."

He was expecting this. Ms. Kowalski had told him she was going to notify his parents about his missing work. He took a seat and braced himself for the bawling out that was coming.

"I received an email from your reading teacher this afternoon," his mother said.

Lonnie hung his head and stared at the table top. "Yeah, I know."

"Why did you tell me that you had finished your project when you knew you hadn't?" she demanded to know.

Refusing to meet her eyes, he shrugged. "I did most of it. Really. And I was going to do the rest of it before class, but time got away from me."

"Ms. Kowalski said that she's deducting ten points from your final grade for each day your project is late. Ten points, Lonnie! Ten points!"

"Mom, I'm going to turn it in tomorrow," he said, finally looking at her. "I promise. I've got some other homework to do, but I'll start—"

"That's not all." She paused and took a deep breath. Her face looked troubled, as if Lonnie's book project was the least of her concerns. He thought she was going to tell him that a friend or family member had died. Or maybe she was going to rag on his dad because he still hadn't found a job.

"I had lunch with Otis Barnaby today," she said. "Lonnie, he wasn't mistaken about what he heard when those kids broke into the warehouse. One boy did call another one Slurpee." She took another long breath, as if talking to him was exhausting her. "Otis also gave me a description of the clothes the three boys were wearing."

Lonnie tried not to show fear, but his insides melted, and he felt as if he might wet his pants. His mother rose from the table and went to the utility room. She returned, holding Lonnie's green polo shirt and blue jeans.

"Are these the clothes you had on yesterday?"

CHAPTER SEVEN

LONNIE HAD MIXED FEELINGS about telling lies. He knew it was wrong to do it. The Bible said he wasn't supposed to lie. On the other hand, lying had helped him get out of some tough spots. When his mother refused to listen to reason after he pleaded with her not to make him go to church, he decided to take matters into his own hands. People might say that by his leading his mother to think he was in church instead of at Catfish Creek, he was lying. But at least it helped preserve the peace at home. He also knew his mother would jump all over him if she learned that he hadn't finished his book project, so he told her he'd done it. That little fib didn't turn out too well, but it was fixable. He could still turn in his project, even if it meant that Ms. Kowalski would take ten points off his final grade.

But if he ever considered getting righteous and truthful, now wasn't the time to start. There was no way he could convince his mother that, yes, he had gone inside the warehouse, but no, he hadn't vandalized it. Too much damage had been done to the place. Plus, the Marsville police had gotten involved.

Lonnie took the green polo shirt from his mother and studied it, furrowing his brows, as if he was thinking hard. "No," he said. "Yesterday, I wore a blue polo shirt. I wore this one to church Sunday. I was going to wear the blue one to church, but it was kind of wrinkled, and I didn't want to ask you to iron it for me, so I wore this green one." Steeling his nerves, he asked, "Why do you want to know what I had on yesterday? Do you think I was one of those kids who broke into the paper company?"

Unfazed, his mother eyed him skeptically. "If you didn't wear this green shirt yesterday, why was it sitting on top of your dirty clothes hamper instead of the blue one?"

Good question. Still, Lonnie didn't let it rattle him. "Oh, well, you see, all my clothes were on the floor, and I knew you were going to do the laundry today, so I picked them up and threw them in the hamper." Shrugging innocently, he added, "I guess my green shirt just ended up on top."

His mother wasn't a cop, but she had been trained to be one, and most times, she could sniff out a lie. "Lonnie, I want you to be truthful with me. Where did you go yesterday?"

Keeping up his deception, he answered, "Um, I spent most of the day here at the house reading my book. I did go out for a little while to see Axel 'cause I wanted him to help me with my project. See, Axel's already read *The Dumfrees Move In*. That's the book I have to read for my class. The story's about this family that lives in Phoenix and Mr. Dumfree's been transferred by his company to Los Angeles, but their house . . . " He paused. "Anyway, Axel said he'd help me with my project."

"And you still couldn't get it done on time?" she scoffed.

"It's just that we started playing with Axel's video games and stuff," Lonnie said, trying to look guilty. "I guess it just got late. After that, I came home."

"Did you and Axel go anywhere?" she persisted.

Lonnie faked a laugh. "Mom, are you kidding? You know Axel's parents. They never let him out of their sight. Remember? They wouldn't let him go to the mall with me even after you talked to them and said you'd take us. No, we just hung out at his house. You can call his mom and ask her if you don't believe me."

He knew she wouldn't call. His mother didn't care for Axel's parents. Lonnie had heard her refer to them as pseudo-intellectual snobs. He wasn't sure what that meant, but he didn't think she was paying them a compliment.

"No, that's fine," she said, although Lonnie had a feeling she wasn't thoroughly convinced. She took his polo shirt and jeans back to the utility room and crammed them into the clothes washer.

"Where's Dad?" Lonnie asked, wondering if she had shared her suspicions with him.

"Who knows?" she said with a roll of her eyes.

She washed her hands in the kitchen sink. Then she took out a package of ground beef, a carton of eggs, an onion and a bottle of ketchup from the fridge, items she had picked up at the grocery store that her husband had neglected to buy the day before.

Feeling satisfied that he had gotten away with his fat lie, Lonnie grabbed an apple from the fruit dish.

"Don't snack too much," his mother said. "Dinner will be ready in about an hour."

"What are we having?"

"Meatloaf with mashed potatoes and green beans."

"M-m-m. I love your meatloaf," Lonnie said. In a way, his praising his mother's meatloaf was his reward to her for believing his story.

He started to leave when his mother stunned him with another shocker. "Listen, Otis is pretty sure that the boys who broke into the warehouse are students from your school. He told me that the big kid, the one called Slurpee, looked old enough to be in high school. But Madison is a little too far from the warehouse, so Otis is sticking with his hunch that the vandals are Wyatt Middle School students. Anyway, he's thinking about going to your school tomorrow to talk to your principal. Otis wants to look through yearbook photos to see if he can identify this Slurpee kid. If he can, maybe the boy will lead him to the others who vandalized the warehouse with him."

Lonnie's knees buckled, and this time he did pee in his pants a little.

They were done for. If Mr. Barnaby showed up at his school, it would take him only minutes before he recognized Herman Gilmore from his yearbook photo. And shortly after that, Lonnie and Axel would be called out of their classrooms to go to the office, where Herman would be sitting with Dr. Lambert, the principal, and Mr. Barnaby, spilling his guts. The second they walked inside the office, Herman would point to them and say, "Yeah, those are the guys who were with me at the warehouse."

Lonnie tried calling Axel, but his cell phone went to automatic voice mail. Didn't he ever charge that thing? He tried Axel's house phone and Daisy picked up.

"Hey, Daisy," Lonnie said, "put Axel on the phone for me, would you?"

He heard a muffled voice in the background to which Daisy replied, "It's *el vago!*"

God, he hated that name.

Axel's mom took the phone. "I'm sorry, Lonnie, but Axel can't talk to you right now. He's got a lot of homework. Would you like to leave him a message?"

Yeah, tell him that the cops are gonna arrest him at school tomorrow for breaking into the Martex warehouse. They're gonna lock him up in jail, and he won't get to go to college 'cause you're gonna kill him.

"No, just tell him to call me as soon as he gets a chance," Lonnie said.

After he hung up, he let himself drop on his bed. How was he going to get out of this? What lie could he possibly come up with to convince his parents and Mr. Barnaby that he hadn't been at the warehouse? He racked his brain for answers but found none. Even if he denied the whole thing and claimed that Herman was making it up, he knew Axel would cave in and start blubbering like an idiot. He'd tell the whole world that they had gone inside the warehouse.

Lonnie once heard someone — Brother Elrod, maybe — say that confession is good for the soul. Perhaps it was time to come clean and finally tell the truth. His mother might not believe that he hadn't caused any of the destruction, but at least she could let Mr. Barnaby know he had been involved. That way, Mr. Barnaby wouldn't need to go to Wyatt Middle School, and Lonnie and Axel and Herman could avoid the embarrassment of being hauled off to jail, handcuffed, in front of everyone.

While he and his mother ate dinner, he thought of worse-case scenarios. They were kids, so he didn't think the police would put them in jail. But their parents would have to pay for the damages, even though he and Axel weren't responsible for any of it. After all, they couldn't prove that they hadn't busted the windows and trashed the office.

Axel's parents would undoubtedly forbid their son from ever hanging out with *el vago* again. They would say Lonnie was a bad influence and that Axel needed to make other friends. Lonnie would be grounded for at least a month. His parents would take the TV out of his bedroom, and he wouldn't be able to leave the house for anything, except to go to school and church. As a personal punishment to himself, Lonnie decided he would remain in the sanctuary on Sunday mornings to hear Brother Elrod preach and not sneak off to Catfish Creek.

≈ ≈ ≈

He completed the written portion of his book project without calling Axel for help. All he needed now was to redraw the cover for *The Dumfrees Move In.* He spread out colored pencils, crayons and markers on the kitchen table and had just begun sketching his picture when his mother came in to say goodbye.

"Be sure to tell your father about the meatloaf. It's in the fridge. And after he eats, tell him I said for him to put his dirty dishes in the dishwasher and to turn on the machine."

Lonnie couldn't put it off any longer. She had to know the truth. On rubbery legs, he rose from his chair and said softly, "Mom, there's something I have to tell you."

She glanced up at the wall clock. "Well, make it quick. I'm running late as it is."

"It's about what happened at the paper company yesterday," he said and swallowed hard.

"What about it?"

"Me and Axel and a kid named Herman . . . we were there."

His mother regarded him coldly. "Are you telling me that you were the ones who vandalized the warehouse?"

"Not me. Or Axel. It was Herman . . . we call him Slurpee . . . who did all that stuff."

"You broke into the warehouse?" she shrieked.

"Yeah, but me and Axel didn't do anything. Honest, Mom. We went inside the warehouse, but Slurpee . . . I mean, Herman, was the one who busted the windows. He was the one who—"

"You broke into the warehouse?" his mother repeated, seething with contempt. "I can't believe what I'm hearing!" She clapped her hands over her head. "My God, what's happened to you, Lonnie? You don't do anything in school. You don't help out around the house. You can't even keep your room clean. And now you're telling me you're out on the streets, vandalizing!"

"I didn't—"

"Are you on drugs?"

"Mom, it's not like that. I promise."

She looked up at the wall clock again. "I can't talk about this right now. I have to go to work."

"Let me call you on your cell and explain what happened."

"No! I don't want to discuss this over the phone." She looked at him disgustedly. "I don't know who you are anymore. I can't trust you. Everything that comes out of your mouth is a lie!" She sniffled and wiped away a tear. "I have to go."

She stalked out of the house, ignoring the rain. In her anger, she had forgotten to take her umbrella.

"Be safe," Lonnie whispered as he watched her leave.

After she was gone, he finished his book cover. Lonnie had a talent for drawing, and he had intended to design a really cool cover, with lots of details, but his heart was no longer in it. Anyway, he doubted Ms. Kowalski would give him extra credit for a well-drawn cover. The picture was the least important part of the project. It was something his teacher had assigned so the dummies in Progressive Reading could feel like they had accomplished something special.

At around ten, Lonnie's dad came home with his breath reeking of alcohol. Since he didn't mention anything about the Martex warehouse, Lonnie guessed that his mother was saving that bit of news for him until she returned home from work. He told him about the meatloaf. His dad took it out of the fridge and zapped it in the microwave. Then he took his food to the den to eat while he watched TV.

With his project, as well as the rest of his homework finally finished, Lonnie packed everything in his backpack. He tried calling Axel on his cell to let him know that he had told his mother about the break-in but got no answer.

He wasn't ready to go to bed yet, so he went to the den to watch TV with his dad. He found him passed out on the couch, snoring loudly. His dad had been watching *I* ♡ *(To Eat) NY*, a movie about a group of people who hole up inside the New York Public Library to escape an attacking mob of zombies.

On TV, the zombies walked aimlessly up and down the steps of the library, without any purpose other than to find food for their flesh-starved appetites. Other zombies crawled on top of the sculpture lions that graced the entrance.

The movie had been running on HBO, and Lonnie had already seen it, so he knew how it was going to end. The zombies would eventually break down the library doors and kill all the survivors inside. Axel was right. Zombie movies do tend to have the same basic plot.

Immediately following *I ♡ (To Eat) NY*, a romantic comedy called *Begin Again, Again* came on. Lonnie turned off the TV and went to bed, leaving his dad asleep on the couch.

He dreamed he was back at the warehouse, running through the paper labyrinth. The guard-thing, with its decaying flesh, chased after him. But no matter how fast Lonnie ran, the guard-thing seemed to be directly behind him.

"La-a-a-a-ne-e-e-e!" it called in a sickly voice. *"I'm gonna getcha, La-ne-e-e-e!"*

Straight, then right, then left, Lonnie zigzagged. He looked back for a second. The guard-thing was nearly on top of him, opening and closing its jaws.

Left, right, left, left, Lonnie ran, gasping for air.

"I'm right behind you, La-ne-e-e-e!"

He could feel the guard-thing's hot breath, which smelled like rotten eggs, burning his neck. Faster he ran, faster, faster, until he felt he would collapse from exhaustion.

Up ahead he saw a bright, almost blinding light. He knew that if he could just reach it, he would be safe. With every ounce of strength left in his legs, he raced toward the light.

Suddenly, the guard-thing appeared in front of him, grinning a mouthful of yellow-brown, death teeth.

"Gotcha!"

With one hand, it seized him by his shirt. With the other, it pulled out its gun. Then Lonnie heard a shot.

" —shot!"

His eyes snapped open and he looked around, disoriented. The ceiling light was on, and his dad was standing next to his bed, shaking him.

"Lonnie! Wake up! Wake up! It's your mom. She's been shot!"

CHAPTER EIGHT

FOR A SECOND, LONNIE THOUGHT he was still dreaming, but the look of horror on his dad's face told him otherwise.

"She caught a guy breaking into a car. He . . . he had a gun and . . . oh, God!" Lonnie's dad shuddered and began to sob. "Get your clothes on. We've gotta get to the hospital."

Lonnie sat up in his bed, hardly believing what he was hearing. "Somebody shot Mom?"

"I'll tell you about it when we get in the car." His dad grabbed Lonnie's pants and shirt from the floor and tossed them to him. "Come on, get dressed. We've gotta go!"

Lonnie hopped out of bed and put on his clothes. Outside his room, he could hear his dad talking on the phone.

"I don't know how bad she's hurt. She's been taken to Landry Memorial. Yeah, me and Lonnie are heading out there right now. Okay, see you there."

They jumped in the Suburban and drove to the hospital, with Lonnie's dad ignoring the speed limits and traffic lights. At two o'clock in the morning, though, few cars were on the highway and there were no cops around.

On the way, Lonnie's dad explained that he had gotten a call from Clifford Jenkins, Lonnie's mother's supervisor, who told him that while she was patrolling the parking lot, she spotted a man removing a stereo from a car, so she confronted him. Without warning, the man pulled out a gun and fired. She never had a chance to draw her weapon.

"Dad, Mom's going to be okay, isn't she?" Lonnie asked out of a dry throat.

"Yeah, 'course she is. Your mom's tough. She's gonna be fine. You . . . you'll see."

Lonnie knew his dad was trying to reassure him, but he didn't sound convincing. He sniffled and wept so much, Lonnie was afraid he was going to wreck the car before they reached the hospital.

Twenty minutes later, they arrived at Landry Memorial and rushed to the emergency room triage desk.

"My wife is Rebecca Rodríguez," Lonnie's dad told the nurse. "She's a security guard. She was shot. Where is she, and is she all right?"

The nurse looked up the name on her computer. Then she said, "I'm sorry, sir, but I can't give out that information. Please have a seat. Someone will come and talk to you shortly."

"But she's my wife!" Lonnie's dad yelled, slamming his hand on the desk. "I have a right to know how she is."

"Sir, please sit down," the nurse said curtly. "Somebody will be with you in a moment."

He glared at her, but she turned away and continued working. Realizing he wasn't going to get any more information out of her, he and Lonnie looked for a place to sit.

Lonnie couldn't believe how many people were in the emergency waiting room at that hour—fifty maybe. Many of them had their eyes closed and appeared to have been there a long time. A lady had her head bandaged up, and she looked like she was wearing a turban. A guy was hunched over, holding his stomach and moaning. Another guy sitting in the row in front of them had his head tilted back. He smelled of alcohol and vomit.

Clifford Jenkins arrived a few minutes later. "How's Becky?" he asked.

"I don't know," Lonnie's dad said. "That idiot nurse won't tell me nothing. How did she look to you, Cliff?"

Mr. Jenkins sat down. He stared at Lonnie, unsure whether he should say anything in front of him.

"Lonnie, go over there by the nurse's desk for a minute, would you?" his dad said.

"No, I want to hear about Mom."

His dad hesitated, then nodded an *okay* to Mr. Jenkins.

"Becky was shot once at close range," Mr. Jenkins said. "But she managed to radio me for help. When I found her, she was lucid enough to tell me what happened. She also gave me a description of the perp, which I've already shared with the police." Mr. Jenkins cleared his throat, then continued. "She passed out soon after that, before the paramedics arrived." He cleared his throat again. "I'm going to be real honest with you, Richard. Becky lost a lot of blood."

Lonnie's insides lurched, and he felt as if he was going to puke. He hurried to the bathroom. With his head hanging over the toilet, he dry heaved a couple of times, but nothing came out. He remained there a little longer just to make sure. Then he tore off a strip of tissue paper and blew his nose.

When he came out of the bathroom, he saw his grandparents Salinas, who had just arrived, talking with his dad and Mr. Jenkins. His uncles, Rubén and Beto, soon joined them. They tried to get more information from the triage nurse, but all she did was repeat what she had already told Lonnie and his dad.

Things grew testy when Mr. Jenkins suggested that Lonnie's mother had been shot because she hadn't followed proper procedures. "If she had called 911 instead of trying to nab the perp herself, this might not have happened."

"So you're telling us this is Becky's fault?" Lonnie's grandpa asked irately.

"No, Arthur. All I'm saying is that company policy states that . . . "

"I don't give a damn about your company policy!" Lonnie's grandpa retorted. "Becky was shot in the line of duty, and right now she's fighting for her life. How dare you try to put the blame on her. It seems to me like you're more concerned about your company than you are about my daughter!"

People turned and stared at them. The drunk guy sitting in front of them woke up and looked around, dazed, as if wondering where he was.

Uncle Beto took his father by the arm. "Papi, calm down," he said. "Nobody's blaming anyone. Mr. Jenkins is just as concerned about Becky as we are. We're tired, that's all. Tired and scared. Instead of arguing, we need to be praying that she's going to be all right."

A half hour later, a uniformed Marsville police officer and a man in a suit approached them. "Are you here for Rebecca Rodríguez?" the man in the suit asked.

Lonnie's grandpa told him they were.

"I'm Detective Samuel Olsen with the Crimes Against Persons Unit," the man said.

"What's that?" Lonnie asked.

Detective Olsen looked at him, as if he hadn't noticed him before. "Crimes Against Persons is, um . . . well, anytime a person's been assaulted . . . shot, stabbed, or beaten . . . we're sent to investigate it."

"How's my wife?" Lonnie's dad asked.

Detective Olsen glanced around. "Let's go somewhere more private."

When he said that, Lonnie realized his mother's condition was so critical, the detective couldn't talk about it in front of the other people in the waiting room.

Detective Olsen escorted them to a small family room and shut the door. "Mrs. Rodríguez received a gunshot wound to the chest," he said, pointing to his heart area. "She's in surgery right now, and the doctors are doing everything they can for her. That's all I can tell you about her condition at this time."

The uniformed officer looked at the detective, then said, "I don't know if this is any consolation to you folks, but I think you should be aware that our patrol division has apprehended a suspect."

"Who is it?" Lonnie's grandpa asked, wondering if the suspect was someone he had dealt with when he worked for the Marsville P.D.

"His name is Kevin Williams," Detective Olsen answered for the uniformed officer. "He's served time in the county jail for a number of offenses. From what we understand, he's confessed to shooting Mrs. Rodríguez. Right now he's being held for aggravated assault, but that charge could change if . . . " He caught himself. "Well, let's just hope Mrs. Rodríguez pulls through."

He introduced the uniformed officer as John Zúñiga. "I'll be in contact with you. But in the meanwhile, Officer Zúñiga is going to take you upstairs to the surgery floor, where you can wait until the doctors let you know how Mrs. Rodríguez is doing."

≈   ≈   ≈

They rode the elevator to the second floor. Officer Zúñiga took them to another family room, where they waited, while he stood outside the door.

There were no windows in the room, and Lonnie felt cramped and claustrophobic. While everyone tried to fill the time by making idle chit-chat, he stepped out of the room. He walked down the hallway to the double doors at the end, knowing his mother was somewhere on the other side, being treated by the doctors. Standing there, something Jo Marie said earlier came to him.

"I will execute terrible vengeance against them to punish them for what they have done."

The Bible verse made Lonnie wonder: *Is God punishing me for sneaking out of church? For lying? For breaking into the warehouse? Is this why He allowed my mom to get shot? Is this my fault?*

A heavy weight of guilt overcame him, and he began to cry. Officer Zúñiga looked in his direction, and then out of respect, turned away. Lonnie returned to the bathroom and washed his face. Afterward, he rejoined his family and Mr. Jenkins.

From time to time, he peered down the hallway at the double doors, wishing the doctors would hurry and tell them that his mother was going to be all right.

Shortly, a hospital chaplain walked out of the elevator. Accompanying him was a large man, the size of a pro football linebacker, wearing a brown sports jacket and a tie.

The big man peeked inside the waiting room. Then he called Officer Zúñiga away from the door. While they talked, a doctor and a nurse came out of the double doors and huddled with them.

They were discussing his mother, Lonnie was sure of it. And by the expressions on their faces, things didn't look good. When they were done, the five of them entered the waiting room and gathered around the family.

The big man shut the door and said, "I'm Detective Paul Campbell with the Marsville Police Homicide Division."

Lonnie's dad wrapped an arm around his son and drew him close.

"As you know, Rebecca Rodríguez suffered a severe gunshot wound and was rushed over here by the paramedics," Detective Campbell said. "The doctors worked on her the best they could, but . . . " He sighed. "But ultimately, they couldn't save her. I'm sorry to tell you this. Rebecca passed away a few minutes ago."

CHAPTER NINE

THE DOCTOR EXPLAINED that Lonnie's mother had been shot with a .38 caliber handgun. The bullet penetrated her chest wall, damaged her left lung and pierced the aorta, causing massive blood loss. He went into other details, but Lonnie was too numb to listen. All he knew was that his mother was dead. Beyond that, nothing mattered. The nurse told them they could view the body if they wished, which everyone agreed they wanted to do.

Detective Campbell informed them that the news media was aware of the shooting and had been waiting outside the hospital to hear from the family, but they weren't under any obligation to speak to them. After that, he and Officer Zúñiga left.

The chaplain shared words of sympathy and led them in a prayer. Then he and the nurse took Lonnie and his family to the viewing room, which was similar to the room they had been in, with a couch and chairs. A glass panel, like those found in museum displays, allowed them to see into the next room, where Lonnie's mother's body lay on a gurney. She was encased in a white plastic bag, zipped up to her neck, leaving only her face exposed.

Her hair had been tied in a bun when she left the house. It now hung loosely on the sides of her head. Her eyes were shut, and her mouth turned downward, as if she was sad. Sad that she had been shot. Sad that she was dead. Sad that she wouldn't be going home.

Lonnie's dad and grandma broke into tears, but his grandpa sat stone-face, his lips tight, his chin jutting out. He had been a sergeant in the Marines and had retired from the police force as a lieutenant, so he wasn't easily ruffled. Still, although he didn't show it, Lonnie knew his grandpa had to be hurting inside. After all, that was his only daughter lying lifeless on the gurney. Lonnie's uncles, like his grandpa, sat rigid and expressionless.

Lonnie tried to be strong like them, but tears streamed down his eyes, and his chest felt heavy, as the realization sank in that he would never see his mother alive again. She would never knock on his bedroom door to make sure he was awake and getting ready for school. She would never fix him Saturday pancakes. He would never get to hold her and tell her he loved her.

It occurred to him that he couldn't remember the last time he had told his mother he loved her.

When he was little, she had taught him to say, *I love you, Mommy.* "Say, I love you, Mommy," she would encourage him. And obediently Lonnie would repeat, "I love you, Mommy."

But as he grew older, he felt it was uncool to say that anymore. The best he could muster whenever his mother said she loved him was, "Yeah, me, too." Now he wished more than anything that she could hear him utter those four words again: *I love you, Mommy.*

Lonnie wondered what went through her mind as she lay on the ground in the apartment complex parking lot, the rain pelting down on her, washing away the blood as it drained out of her body. Did she think of him? Did she say, "I love you, Lonnie?"

He hung his head in shame, knowing her last thoughts of him were that he was a vandal and a liar. That he was lazy and irresponsible.

"I don't know who you are anymore. I can't trust you. Everything that comes out of your mouth is a lie."

Just once, Lonnie wished he had done something that would have made her proud of him. Something that would have made her want to stand up and say to the world, "Look everybody! That's my son!"

But he had never accomplished anything outstanding or praiseworthy. He was a nobody, a do-nothing. He was a crummy student. He didn't play sports. *You know what they say, no pass, no play.* He wasn't in the band. He didn't belong to any school organizations. He didn't even go to church, although he had led his mother to believe he did.

Liar, liar, pants on fire!

That's a sin, and you're going to have to answer to the Lord for it.

He buried his face in his hands and wept bitterly. This whole experience felt surreal, like another crazy nightmare. Except that he could wake up from a bad dream. But how was he supposed to wake up from reality? His mother hadn't been attacked by a zombie or a vampire or some other fantasy creature. A real live monster had pulled out a gun and shot her, leaving her lying on the ground, bleeding to death.

When they left the hospital, reporters flocked around them, microphones in hand, bombarding them with questions about the shooting. Lonnie's dad started to respond, but his father-in-law stopped him. He told the reporters that the family wasn't ready to comment yet.

It was almost five o'clock by the time Lonnie and his dad arrived home. His dad turned on the TV to the

Channel 4 news. A weather update was airing. It was followed by a brief traffic report and a commercial break.

The morning broadcast returned with dramatic music and a BREAKING NEWS headline. The anchorwoman, Leticia Reyes, opened the five o'clock segment with a live report of the fatal shooting at the Sherwood Forest Apartments. Scott Harris, one of the reporters who had approached the family, appeared onscreen. With the Landry Memorial Hospital in the background, he recounted the events that led to the tragedy.

Along with the report, Channel 4 showed a photo of the suspect, Kevin Williams. He was twenty-nine years old and had been in and out of jail since he was fifteen, for offenses that included assault, car theft, burglary, evading arrest and drug possession. Now it appeared that his criminal history would include murder.

Kevin Williams looked like he could still pass for fifteen. His height and weight weren't revealed, but Lonnie guessed he stood no taller than five-seven, and weighed around a hundred fifty pounds. His blond hair was long and stringy. He had a pencil-thin mustache, or what the guys at school called peach fuzz. A tiny tuft of hair, like the bristles on an artist's paint brush, grew below his bottom lip.

The reporter mentioned that Kevin Williams was a resident at the Sherwood Forest Apartments, which made Lonnie wonder if his mother had recognized him. Is that why he shot her? So she wouldn't be able to identify him? Next, they showed a clip of Kevin Williams, in handcuffs, being led into the Marsville City Jail by several police officers.

Lonnie's dad bolted from the couch and screamed at the television, "Do you realize what you've done, you worthless piece of trash? You've destroyed my family! You took away my Becky! You . . . " His words faded away in his sobs.

Throughout the day, the phone rang almost non-stop, with friends and relatives calling to express their condolences. Lonnie also received texts from some of his classmates, letting him know how sorry they were to hear about his mother. Word about her death had reached his school, for which he was glad, since his dad hadn't called the office to let them know why he wouldn't be in class. Lonnie was disappointed that he hadn't heard from Axel. But knowing him, his phone probably wasn't charged.

Brother Elrod stopped by. He told Lonnie and his dad that he had been stunned by the news and wanted to extend his deepest sympathies. He also said that the Winfield Road Presbyterian Church was available for the funeral service if they wished to use it, and that he was willing to preside over the service if they needed him. Lonnie's dad told him arrangements hadn't been made yet, but that he would let him know.

Another unannounced visit came from Mr. Barnaby and his wife. Mrs. Barnaby had baked a chicken casserole and a tray of brownies for them. During their visit, Mr. Barnaby gave no hint that he recognized Lonnie as one of the boys from the warehouse, nor did he say anything about having gone to Wyatt Middle School.

After they left, Lonnie's grandparents Salinas showed up. Lonnie's grandma brought a pot of *caldo de res*, a Mexican beef soup, and a package of corn tortillas. His dad told her about Mrs. Barnaby's casserole and that they had planned to have it for lunch, but she ignored him and removed four bowls from the cabinet to serve the *caldo*.

While they ate, Lonnie's grandpa discussed preliminary funeral plans he had made. "I want Socorro to write Becky's obituary," he said. "Socorro teaches English, so she ought to be able to write something good." He creased his brows. "And Richard, I want Beto to be the official spokesperson for the family, you hear? If you get any calls from the media, you give them Beto's number and tell them to talk to him."

Lonnie's dad nodded dutifully. Still, it irritated him that his father-in-law was insinuating that he wasn't capable of talking to reporters without saying something inappropriate.

He told his in-laws about Brother Elrod's offer. Lonnie's grandpa said he would take it into consideration and then continued laying out his plans for the funeral, without giving Lonnie's dad an opportunity to make other suggestions.

"Do you have Becky's insurance papers?" he asked. "I want to go over them to see what kind of coverage she has."

Lonnie's dad wiped his hands on his lap. "Becky, um . . . well, she always handled the money, and, um . . . "

"I think I know where they are," Lonnie said. "Mom keeps all the important papers in a brown metal box in the study closet."

As he stood, he realized he should have said *kept*, not *keeps*. His mother wouldn't be keeping anything in the brown metal box anymore. Lonnie returned with the box, and his grandpa rummaged through it until he found the insurance policy.

"It's not much," he said, sounding disappointed. "Hopefully, it'll be enough to cover the cost of the funeral."

Late that afternoon, Lonnie finally heard from Axel. He apologized for not having called earlier, saying he had left his phone at home. He told Lonnie how sorry he was to hear about his mother. "My whole family is," he said, although Lonnie couldn't imagine Axel's parents caring anything about *el vago*.

He told Axel about Mr. Barnaby's suspicions and asked if he had shown up at school. Axel said he didn't think so. Then he started yammering about how they were going to get in big trouble. But after everything Lonnie had gone through, Mr. Barnaby was the least of his worries.

He and his dad watched the five o'clock evening news. It opened with the story of the shooting. This time, Channel 4 showed a photo of Lonnie's mother that his dad had emailed to the station. It was a Glamour Shots photograph she had gotten made the year before. In it, she smiled coyly, holding the collar of her glittery black jacket to her chin. Lonnie thought she looked incredibly beautiful. Still, he wished his dad hadn't sent in that particular photo. His mother had been murdered, but the picture made her look as if she was going to a party.

The news also aired a clip of a press conference Lonnie's uncle Beto held outside his house, with Lonnie's grandpa and Uncle Rubén standing beside him. Uncle Beto thanked the Marsville Police Department for their outstanding efforts in apprehending the suspect. He also called for justice and swift action against the man who took his sister's life.

Lonnie's dad griped about being left out of the press conference. "Becky was my wife. I belong there with them."

Lonnie wasn't surprised that his dad hadn't been included in the press conference, or that his grandpa hadn't allowed him to help with the funeral plans. His grandpa had often been critical of Lonnie's dad, accusing him of lacking ambition. During one of their many confrontations, he told his son-in-law that a real man wouldn't sit at home doing nothing, while his wife worked to support him.

That night, Lonnie dreamed about his mother. She lay on a gurney, zipped up in a body bag. All of a sudden, she opened her eyes and sat up. She turned and grinned . . .

No! He shoved the image out of his mind. He refused to think of her that way, not even in a nightmare.

CHAPTER TEN

THE FUNERAL SERVICE WAS HELD the following Monday at the Winfield Road Presbyterian Church. Lonnie's dad had wanted to have it earlier, but the service had to wait until an autopsy report and a police investigation could be completed.

Lonnie couldn't believe the number of students from his school that showed up. He learned later that his principal, Dr. Lambert, had sent a letter home, notifying parents that, with their permission, students would be allowed to leave school early to attend the service.

Axel and his family sat a few rows behind him. Across them were some of the other guys—Noe, José and Fernando. Lonnie was glad to see Yvette. She sat in a back pew with Jo Marie and Patricia.

Herman Gilmore didn't make it, for which Lonnie was thankful. Mr. Barnaby and his wife were in attendance, and he was afraid that if Mr. Barnaby saw Herman, he might recognize him.

The temperature outside had climbed to well over a hundred degrees, and the sanctuary was hot and muggy. Lonnie loosened his tie and undid the top button of his shirt. His grandma had bought him the tie and a sports coat for the funeral because he didn't have any dressy clothes to wear.

Lonnie's grandparents Salinas sat with him in the front pew, along with his dad, his grandparents Rodríguez, and his uncles, Rubén and Beto. Other relatives, many of them whose names Lonnie didn't know, sat behind them.

In front of the church, his mother's casket lay atop a metal trolley, surrounded by floral wreaths and photographs. His grandpa had picked out a rose-colored casket to match the pink dress Lonnie's mother would be buried in. Lonnie's dad had suggested that maybe she should be dressed in one of her security uniforms, but his father-in-law balked at the idea and answered him with an emphatic *no!*

Minutes before the service began, Gilly Sandoval, Joe Lara and Mario Hernández showed up with their guitars and an accordion. Lonnie's grandpa had words with his son-in-law for not informing him ahead of time that Los Brujos were going to take part in the service. Nevertheless, he agreed to let them perform.

After an opening greeting and a prayer by Brother Elrod, Lonnie's dad joined Gilly, Joe and Mario onstage to sing "How Great Thou Art." They were followed by Lonnie's cousin Socorro's reading of the obituary she had written for *The Marsville Monitor*.

Another cousin, Amanda, read Psalm twenty-three and afterward, led the congregation in prayer.

While everyone had their heads bowed, Lonnie glanced back to see who else was in attendance. His heart jumped when he thought he saw the guard-thing from his dreams standing against a wall, grinning and waving at him. But it turned out to be a regular Wyndham Security guard who was holding up his hand and mouthing his own prayer.

Tim Beasley, the church music director, asked the congregation to rise for the singing of "Great is Thy Faithfulness."

Lonnie had no desire to sing. He didn't even pick up a hymn book. From where he stood, he could see inside the casket and it tore him up to see his mother in there. It also made him angry. Why did God have to take her away from him? If it was to punish him, couldn't He have come up with something less severe? Was God that heartless? If He needed another soul for His collection, why couldn't He have taken someone like Moses, the homeless guy? Moses served no purpose in life other than to hang out by the I-27 bridge and pester people for money. Or God could have taken Lonnie's science teacher, Mr. Malone, who already looked like walking death.

Great is Thy faithfulness!
Great is Thy faithfulness!
Morning by morning new mercies I see.
All I have needed Thy hand hath provided;
Great is Thy faithfulness, Lord, unto me!

The longer the hymn went, the angrier Lonnie grew toward God. If His faithfulness was so great, why was his mother lying dead in the casket?

Uncle Beto delivered the eulogy. He told funny stories about growing up with his sister, how when they were little, she used to put dresses and make-up on him, as if he was her toy doll. He talked about his sister's sense of humor and how she loved to tell jokes. He spoke about her marriage and how much she loved Richard, which Lonnie thought was weird for him say, because Uncle Beto couldn't stand his brother-in-law. He also talked about his sister's love for Lonnie and how much he meant to her. He mentioned her dedication to her job and the numerous commendations she had earned. Uncle Beto concluded his eulogy by saying, "Not only have I lost my sister, I've also lost one of my best friends."

Lonnie couldn't help but think that if Uncle Beto could see all those wonderful qualities, why couldn't God? Why did He decide: *Sorry, lady, the world doesn't need someone like you.*

By the time Brother Elrod got up to preach, Lonnie's eyes were filled with tears, not just of grief but also of rage. Brother Elrod looked around the room and studied each mourner's face. Placing both hands on the pulpit, he leaned into the microphone, and in an authoritative voice asked, "Is there balm in Gilead?"

Lonnie had no idea where Gilead was, nor did he care if it had any balm in it. And he especially didn't want to hear anymore about God's grace and mercy. What he really wanted to do was to run out of the sanctuary and flee to Catfish Creek, but he couldn't. So he sat and listened to Brother Elrod preach about the balm in Gilead. Or was it a bomb that was in Gilead? He didn't care.

After the service, people came up to hug him and to offer words of compassion. Lonnie realized they meant well, but he didn't find any comfort in hearing that his mother was in a better place, or that her death was somehow part of God's plan. If his mother's death was part of God's plan, then as far as Lonnie was concerned, God's plan stunk.

Jo Marie wrapped her arms around Lonnie's neck and said, "Please know that my prayers are with you."

He peeled her off and asked, "Can your prayers bring back my mom?"

"Uh, well, no. What I meant . . . "

"If they can't, then they aren't any good, are they?"

"Lonnie, Jo Marie was only trying to be nice," her friend Patricia said.

"Sure she was. Just like she was trying to be nice when she told me that God was going to execute terrible vengeance against me." Lonnie sneered at Jo Marie and asked, "Are you happy now? Are you thrilled that God punished me by killing my mom?"

Patricia gasped. "Lonnie, God didn't have anything to do with what happened to your mom. It could've happened to anyone."

"That's okay, Pat," Jo Marie said. "Lonnie's hurting right now. He didn't mean anything by it." She squeezed his hand. "I'll be praying for you."

Lonnie and his family drove in a procession to Pineview Cemetery. They didn't get to ride in a limo because, in trying to keep the costs down, his grandpa hadn't ordered one.

The September sun beat down on them unmercifully. Lonnie was burning up in his coat, but his grandma refused to let him take it off. He was thankful that his Sunday school teacher, Mrs. Finley, had thought to bring water bottles to the cemetery, and she and her husband handed them out as people arrived.

A green tent and chairs were set up at the gravesite, and Lonnie sat between his grandparents Salinas in the front row. Six men, whom he was told were his great uncles, but he couldn't recall ever having met, carried his mother's casket from the hearse and placed it on top of a lowering device in front of the tent.

Once again, Lonnie's dad and Los Brujos performed an impromptu piece, this time a Spanish song titled, "*En las manos del Ser Divino.*"

Brother Elrod read from the book of Romans. He preached a short sermon, and then led everyone in prayer. When he was done, a couple of workers from the Pineview Cemetery lowered the casket, and everyone in attendance was given an opportunity to sprinkle soil from a container into the grave.

With tears in his eyes, Lonnie scooped a handful of dirt and whispered, "I love you, Mommy," before dropping the soil into the ground.

They returned to the church, where some of the ladies had prepared a meal. Lonnie walked around the fellowship hall to get reacquainted with some relatives he hadn't seen in a long time. He met up with Enrique, a cousin his age. What Lonnie remembered most about him was that when Enrique was little, he was so bony, his ribcage protruded from his body. He always smelled of urine and seemed to have a permanent dirt ring around his neck.

Now, Enrique stood five-feet eight and weighed a hundred seventy pounds. He didn't have a dirt ring around his neck, and the only smell Lonnie detected from him was cologne. Enrique attended Red Adair Middle School in Abilene, where he played wide receiver on their football team.

Lonnie was telling him about how he hoped to play football some day when a shouting match erupted behind them. He turned and saw his dad and his grandpa Salinas arguing.

"But you don't have a job, Richard. How are you going to support Lonnie if you don't work?"

Hearing his name, Lonnie left Enrique and made his way toward them.

"He's not gonna live with you, Arthur. You hear me? Lonnie's my boy. He belongs with me."

"What's going on?" Lonnie asked.

"Your grandpa doesn't think I can take care of you," his dad said.

"All I'm saying is that it would be better for Lonnie if he came to live with us until you can find a job."

"No! I'm his father. He needs to be with me. That's the way Becky would've wanted it."

Lonnie's grandfather stepped back and crossed his arms. "Are you sure about that, Richard?" he asked smugly. "Are you really sure that's what Becky would've wanted?"

"What are you getting at?"

"Did you know Becky was planning to leave you?"

"What?"

That revelation jolted Lonnie as much as it did his dad, although it shouldn't have. His parents had been squabbling for years, and he figured it was just a matter of time before something like this happened.

"That's right. She discussed it with Lourdes and me. Becky said she wanted to divorce you, and she asked us if she and Lonnie could stay at our house until she found a new place to live."

"That's a lie!" Lonnie's dad shouted. "Becky loved me. Even Beto said so. Are you gonna tell me that he lied in front of God and all those people when he talked about how much she loved me?"

His father-in-law nudged his chin in the direction of his wife, who was sitting nearby, watching. "Ask Lourdes. She'll tell you."

"This is low, Arthur," Lonnie's dad said in a guttural voice. "This is really low. I just lost my wife, and Lonnie lost his mother. And now you wanna make things worse by trying to split us up? Well, I'm not gonna let you do it. You're not taking Lonnie away from me."

"What do you plan to do for money then? How are you going to support him?"

"That's none of your business!"

"I'm making it my business, Richard. And if I find out that my grandson isn't being taken care of properly, I'll sue you, if I have to, for custody. You better believe it."

Lonnie's dad wrapped an arm around his son's shoulders. "Come on, buddy. Let's get outta here." Before leaving, he glared at his father-in-law and uttered something Lonnie didn't catch. It was just as well. He probably didn't need to hear what he said.

CHAPTER ELEVEN

TUESDAY, LONNIE RETURNED TO SCHOOL. All day, teachers and students approached him, offering their condolences, repeating the same things he had heard a million times: "You're in my thoughts. You're in my prayers. You're in my thoughts and prayers, blah, blah, blah." After a while, he was sick of all the attention and wished everyone would leave him alone.

With the exception of Yvette Sosa.

As soon as he entered Texas history class, she greeted him with a hug and a kiss on the cheek. Ordinarily, that kind of display would have elicited silly howls from the guys. But it was understood that there was nothing romantic about Yvette's affections.

"I wanted to talk to you at the funeral, but there were so many people around you that I didn't get a chance," she said. "But please know how sorry I am about what happened to your mom."

Their conversation was cut short by the bell, and they took their seats. Lonnie thought that maybe after class, he and Yvette could walk down the hallway together. But as soon as Texas history ended, she left with her friends, and Lonnie headed to math class alone.

While Mrs. Ridley demonstrated on the board how to divide with decimals, a girl walked into the room with a note for Lonnie to report to Ms. Hoffman, the guidance counselor.

Oh, great. Someone else who's going to tell me how sorry she is to hear about my loss.

Lonnie didn't have a problem meeting with Ms. Hoffman, though. She was young, probably no older than twenty-five or twenty-six. And pretty, with long, dark-brown hair and deep blue eyes. At the beginning of the school year, she helped Lonnie register for classes, and he found her to be pleasant and easy to talk to.

When he knocked on her door, however, it was the school's other counselor, Mr. Bigelow, who opened it. Lonnie had never met him before, but he had seen him around. Mr. Bigelow was a short, roly-poly man, who reminded Lonnie of Tweedledum and Twiddledee. He wore a yellow, short-sleeved shirt with a red paisley tie and purple pants that were hitched up to his chest, covering his enormous belly.

"Good morning, Lon," he said. "I'm Mr. Bigelow. Come on in."

"Where's Ms. Hoffman?" Lonnie asked, looking around for her. He had never been inside her office, which looked more like a living room. There was a sofa with end tables and lamps on each side, a loveseat and two overstuffed chairs. A tall, wide bookcase stood behind the couch, with books, photographs and figurines neatly organized in it.

"She's on campus doing other things," Mr. Bigelow said. "I'm using her office temporarily while mine's being painted. Won't you have a seat, please?" Mr. Bigelow spoke with a lisp, and the words *seat, please* came out as *theet, pleathe*.

"Where do you want me to sit?" Lonnie asked.

Mr. Bigelow swept his hand over the couch and chairs, as if he was a salesman trying to sell him a piece of furniture. "Anywhere you'd like, Lon."

Lonnie took a seat in one of the overstuffed chairs, and Mr. Bigelow sat across from him on the couch. The counselor opened a file folder and skimmed over the information he had gathered.

This wasn't the first time Lonnie had to deal with a grief counselor. When he was in the third grade, counselors from the district's counseling services had gone to his school to talk to the students after Mr. Lee, the crossing guard, was killed. A woman in too big of a hurry ignored the school zone speed limit and hit Mr. Lee with her car as he was helping some kids cross the street.

"Lon Chaney Rodríguez," Mr. Bigelow read aloud. "That's quite an unusual name."

"I was named after a horror film actor," Lonnie told him. "Do you know who Lon Chaney was?"

"Yes, of course. (*Yeth, of courth*). He played the Wolf Man in that old monster picture from the thirties."

"Actually, *The Wolf Man* came out in 1941," Lonnie corrected him. "And it was Lon Chaney Jr. who starred in it, not his father. But Lon Chaney Jr. wasn't a junior, 'cause his real name was Creighton. After his father died, Creighton got into acting and took his father's name. Anyway, I'm named after the original Lon Chaney."

"My goodness, Lon," Mr. Bigelow said, sounding impressed. "You've certainly done a lot of research on your name."

Lonnie shrugged. "My dad told me about him. He loves horror movies. That's why he named me Lon Chaney."

"Did you and your parents enjoy watching horror pictures together, Lon?" Mr. Bigelow asked.

Here we go. Mr. Bigelow doesn't want to know about my name. He's just trying to find a way to get me to talk about my mom.

"Me and my dad watch them. My mom doesn't care . . . My mom didn't care too much for horror movies."

"What sorts of things did you and your momma like to do together, Lon?" Mr. Bigelow asked. "I mean, just the two of you."

"Can you call me Lonnie? That's what everybody calls me."

"Yes, of course . . . Lonnie." Mr. Bigelow sat the file folder down and leaned back with his hands folded over his stomach. "Tell me about your momma. What are some of the best memories you have of her?"

Lonnie shifted uncomfortably in his chair and turned away. He didn't want to discuss his mother with him. Those memories were private. They belonged to him. And to anyone he chose to share them with. They weren't for the taking, just because a counselor asked for them. Thinking about his mother made his eyes well up.

"That's all right, Lon," Mr. Bigelow said gently. He reached for a Kleenex box and offered it to him.

Lonnie took a tissue and wiped his eyes. He collected himself and straightened up. "I'm sorry, sir, but I can't talk about my mom right now. Is it okay if I go back to class? I've missed a lot of assignments, and I really can't afford to be out anymore."

Science class had just started, and Lonnie wasn't particularly looking forward to being in there, but it beat having to pour out his life story to Humpty-Dumpty.

"Your teachers understand that you're going through a grieving period," Mr. Bigelow said. "Don't worry about your grades, Lon. You've got enough on your plate as it is. Your teachers will work with you to make sure you don't fall behind in your studies."

"Yes, sir, I know. But I'm trying to get back into my regular routine."

Mr. Bigelow picked up the file folder and read over his notes again. "There's no need to rush back to your classes, Lon . . . I mean, Lonnie. You're carrying a lot of emotional weight right now, and I'm simply here to help you unload some of it."

What's this joker's problem? Doesn't he get it that I don't want to talk to him?

"I appreciate that, sir," Lonnie said, trying not to sound frustrated. "But I'm fine. Really. Me and my dad are pretty close, and we've talked a lot about what happened."

That was a lie. Ever since his mother died, Lonnie and his dad had hardly spoken to each other. His dad was in mourning, Lonnie realized—they both were—but Lonnie was beginning to grow concerned about him. His dad had begun to slip into a deep funk, and Lonnie didn't know how to get him out of it. All weekend, he sat in front of the TV, staring blankly at it, while downing one beer after another.

"That's good, that's good," Mr. Bigelow said cheerily. "It's important to be close to your daddy, especially at a time like this. Well, if you'd rather go back to class to be with your friends, I'm sure it'll be all right. I'll stop by every once in a while to see how you're doing. In the meantime, feel free to come see me if ever you need anything."

He asked Lonnie where he was supposed to be. Then he escorted him to the science lab.

After class, Lonnie ran into Jo Marie in the hallway. Even though he found her annoying, he felt he needed to apologize for his rude behavior at church.

"That's okay, Lonnie," she said. "I know you didn't mean any of those things. You were hurt and upset. Sometimes when bad things happen to us, we blame God. But instead of blaming God, we need to trust Him. We need to be like Job, who—"

"Please don't preach to me, Jo Marie," Lonnie said. "I'm sorry, but I don't feel like hearing a sermon right now."

She reached into her purse and pulled out a Bible tract. "I want you to read this little booklet when you get a chance. It's filled with really powerful Scriptures that can bring you comfort during this hard time in your life. And when I see you in church Sunday, I'll give you some other materials that can help you better understand the nature of God."

Lonnie took the Bible tract and thanked her, but he had no intention of reading it. He was done with church. With his mother gone, he no longer had to pretend to go there.

At lunch, he asked Axel if Mr. Barnaby had ever shown up at school, and Axel said he hadn't. Lonnie thought perhaps Mr. Barnaby was too distraught to follow up on his hunch. Or maybe he realized he was no longer a cop and shouldn't be conducting investigations on his own. Or he might have decided there were far bigger problems in the world to deal with than a few punk troublemakers.

Lonnie invited Axel to come over to his house after school, thinking that they might hang out at Catfish Creek. "You can tell your parents that since I've missed a lot of school, you're going to help me catch up on my studies."

Axel said he'd call to let him know.

"Make sure your phone's charged," Lonnie told him before they separated to go to fourth period.

In Progressive Reading, he handed his book project to Ms. Kowalski. Although it was almost a week overdue, she accepted it, saying she would give him full credit for his project without deducting any points for late work.

Lonnie should have been grateful, but he didn't care what grade he got. The only reason he turned it in was because he had put his project in his backpack the night his mother died, and it was still in there.

His dad told him that he needed to start doing better in school because it was what his mom would have wanted. He'd never shown any interest before, so Lonnie thought it was lame of him to use her death as an attempt to motivate him to work harder. His mom was gone and nothing Lonnie did was going to change that. He could make straight A's, but that still wouldn't bring her back. Like he told Axel, there's no cure for zombie-ism because there's no cure for death.

CHAPTER TWELVE

AFTER SCHOOL, LONNIE FOUND HIS DAD sprawled on the couch, asleep, with crushed beer cans on the coffee table. He thought that after the argument with his father-in-law, his dad would be out looking for a job, but it didn't appear as if he had left the house all day.

Axel called. He told Lonnie that his parents didn't want him hanging out at his house anymore, now that his mom was gone. What did they think would happen? That Lonnie and his dad would don leatherface masks and chase after Axel with chainsaws? Lonnie was finding it difficult to maintain his friendship with Axel when his parents didn't feel they could trust him.

He went to the kitchen to grab something to snack on, and for a second, he expected to find his mom in there, singing along to a song on the radio.

Fixing dinner would probably fall on him now. His dad's cooking skills were limited to nuking stuff in the microwave, and he wasn't always successful doing that. Lonnie knew how to make scrambled eggs, sandwiches and quesadillas. But he would have to learn how to prepare other meals.

Then there was the housework. His dad had never lifted a finger to do any of it. As a truck driver, he would be gone for days, and he expected the house to be clean when he returned. Sometimes Lonnie helped out by polishing the furniture and sweeping the floor. Now, it appeared that he would have to do all the cleaning, including scrubbing the toilets.

Lonnie also wondered about the wash. Who was going to do that? He had absolutely no idea how to wash clothes. He didn't even know how to turn on the washing machine, and he doubted his dad did, either. Lonnie would have to learn in a hurry. He would also have to figure out how to iron and fold clothes, plus everything else his mom used to do that he and his dad had taken for granted.

All these thoughts burned in Lonnie's mind, and he needed to get out of the house to sort things out.

His dad was still asleep, and nothing short of a nuclear explosion was going to wake him, so Lonnie didn't let him know he was leaving. Anyway, he had his cell phone, and unlike Axel, he always kept it charged. If his dad grew worried about him, he was just a phone call away.

Lonnie crossed the street and headed toward the back of the Winfield Road Presbyterian Church. He climbed over the fence and hiked up the hill to the railroad tracks, then down the other side to Catfish Creek. Having taken this same route countless times, he had formed a walking path in the grass.

Near the bank of the creek, he sat on a boulder and took in the scenery. Minnows blew tiny bubbles in the water as they swam along. Dragonflies flitted back and forth above them. A couple of turtles crawled on a rock to bask in the sun.

Lonnie thought about all the Sundays he had made his mother believe he was in church when the whole time he was out here, playing hookey. Was hookey the right term to use? Can a person play hookey from church, or does that apply only to school?

The first time he came to Catfish Creek was to sneak out of church. But he kept returning because it was the only place where he could truly be alone, where he could meditate and reflect on life. In a way, he felt closer to God out here than he did inside the church.

Lonnie had gotten over his anger toward God, although he still couldn't understand why He had taken away his mother. What was He planning to do with her soul? Lonnie knew what Brother Elrod preached, concerning the hereafter. Still, he was curious about what really happens to people when they die. Do they go to heaven? To hell? To purgatory? Do they become angels? Was his mom now an angel? Had she been issued a harp and a pair of wings? Was she flying around like those dragonflies near the water?

In pictures Lonnie had seen of angels, they usually wore white choir robes with halos encircling their heads. Somehow he couldn't imagine his mom as an angel, unless she was an angel with a gun belt strapped around her waist and a badge on her robe.

She hadn't attended church much, but Lonnie knew she believed in God. When he was little, she had taught him the "God is Great, God is Good" prayer, and he used to recite before he ate. She had also taught him the "Jesus Loves Me" song, which they would sing together. Surely God wouldn't keep his mother out of heaven just because she didn't go to church or read the Bible on a regular basis.

Lonnie had seen a movie—he couldn't remember the name of it—about a guy who died and had been condemned to live on Earth as a ghost, until he could earn a place in heaven by helping a troubled kid turn his life around.

Was that what God had in store for his mom? Was Lonnie that troubled kid? Was she still roaming the Earth as a ghost, watching over him, making sure he didn't muck up his life anymore than it already was?

The sound of rustling leaves startled him.

Lonnie spun around and looked in the direction of the noise. Something was moving through the underbrush, about twenty yards away. At first he thought it might be a feral dog or even a coyote. They'd had problems with coyotes preying on domestic dogs and cats in their neighborhood. Lonnie jumped to his feet and hid behind a tree, fearful of being attacked by a wild animal, with no one knowing where he was. He ventured to poke his head out and saw a skinny man with long, gray hair and a long, gray beard emerge from the underbrush.

Moses! What's he doing here?

The homeless man made his way to the creek bank, where he slipped off his backpack and dropped it on the ground. He rolled up his pants legs, removed his T-shirt and stepped into the water. Stooping, he splashed his face, chest and arm pits. When he was done, he toweled himself with his shirt. He sat down, opened his backpack and took out a water bottle, an apple and a 7-Eleven sandwich.

Lonnie felt like a Peeping Tom watching him, but he didn't know what else to do. If he made any sudden moves, Moses was sure to hear him. Shielded by the tree, he remained a captive audience, hoping Moses would hurry and leave.

When he finished eating, Moses wiped his teeth with his T-shirt. Then he pulled a clean shirt out of his backpack and slipped it on. He gathered his trash and stuffed it into his backpack, which Lonnie thought was commendable. He would have thought that a homeless guy wouldn't care about being a litterbug. Moses stood and stretched his arms, inadvertently turning his face toward Lonnie.

"Hey, I see you! What are you doing, kid? You spying on me?" Moses took a couple of steps, then stopped and motioned for Lonnie to move away from the tree. "C'mere, kid, I wanna talk to you."

The "stranger-danger" sirens sounded in Lonnie's head, and he ran up the hill, ignoring the limbs and overgrown prickly weeds that scratched his face and arms.

Reaching the railroad tracks, he looked back to see if Moses was following him. Thankfully, he wasn't. Lonnie paused to catch his breath. He felt mortified. His private hiding place had been invaded. Moses had taken it over. Or maybe he was the invader. Catfish Creek might have been Moses' home, and Lonnie was the one who had intruded on his privacy. Moses probably slept out there somewhere.

Lonnie didn't know much about homeless people, except for what his dad had told him. He had seen them on major street corners throughout the city, holding cardboard signs that said things like, WILL WORK FOR FOOD or HUNGRY PLEASE HELP or SPARE CHANGE? And each sign ended with GOD BLESS. Sometimes when Lonnie and his parents drove through downtown, he would see homeless people lounging outside the city's shelters, like stray animals.

As shaken as Lonnie was, he couldn't help but be curious about Moses. Had he once been a working stiff, like his dad, with a home and a family? Had he lost his job and was never able to find another one?

Heading home, Lonnie thought about their situation. His parents had seldom discussed money matters with him, but he knew that ever since his dad had gotten fired, they had struggled financially. His mom had never earned much as a security guard, but somehow she had managed to pay the bills, even with his dad's meager unemployment checks. What was going to happen to them now that she was gone, and they could no longer count on her income? His dad would have to find work soon. But what if he couldn't? What if no one hired him?

Lonnie shuddered to think that the same thing that happened to Moses could happen to them.

CHAPTER THIRTEEN

IN THE WEEKS THAT FOLLOWED, Lonnie learned how to make dinner. After reading through a cookbook he had checked out of his school's library, he was able to prepare a number of meals, including baked chicken and mashed potatoes, beef patties and fries, and spaghetti with meat sauce. It wasn't gourmet, but they weren't starving. Breakfast was usually cereal or Eggo waffles. If Lonnie had time, he would fix sausage and eggs.

He even learned how to do the wash. It took a few mishaps, such as turning their white T-shirts and underwear pink, when he mixed colored clothes with white ones, but in time, he got the hang of it.

Lonnie kept the house, including his room, tidy and clean, something that would have shocked his mom. He didn't do it because he thought she was an angel who was trying to steer him in the right direction so she could earn a place in heaven. Mainly he did it because his grandparents popped in one day, unexpectedly, and saw the house in a mess. Appalled, his grandpa threatened to report Lonnie's dad to Child Protective Services.

Lonnie knew his grandparents Salinas loved him and were concerned about his well-being, but there was no way he wanted to live with them. He had been surprised to learn that his mother had considered divorcing his dad and had planned to have Lonnie move in with her at his grandparents' house. Why hadn't she asked him what he thought?

His grandma was okay. She was a gentle, soft-spoken woman, who always welcomed him into their home with a warm hug and a kiss. She laughed at all his jokes, no matter how dumb they were. She never got tired of playing checkers or tic-tac-toe with him, and she always let him win.

His grandpa, on the other hand, could be rough and demanding. He never made a request. Everything was an order.

"Bring me the newspaper. Serve me some coffee. Call the plumber, and tell him I said to hurry it up."

When Lonnie was little, his grandpa would take him outside to play baseball, but it was never fun. He would always yell at Lonnie for any mistake he made. And he made plenty of them.

"You're not keeping your eyes on the ball!"

"Is there something wrong with your arm that you can't throw any harder than that?"

"Stop acting like you're scared of getting hit!"

Lonnie could tell that his dad was intimidated by his father-in-law, so he had to give him his props when he stood up to him the day of the funeral. He may not have been the ideal father, but he was still his dad, and Lonnie was not about to abandon him, especially at a time like this.

The problem was, his dad wasn't making much of an effort to take care of him. He continued to drink, averaging a six-pack a day—more on the weekends. Whenever Lonnie talked to him about trying to stop, he would get defensive and tell him to stay out of his business.

He still hadn't found a regular job. His dad contacted his former boss at Mateo's, the restaurant he once worked at as a waiter, but was told that with the economy being so bad, they couldn't afford to hire anyone. He tried other restaurants and got the same response. Even the fast-food places — McDonald's, Burger King, KFC — all turned him down.

"They want kids working for them, not old guys like me," Lonnie's dad complained.

He did manage to talk Gilly Sandoval, Joe Lara and Mario Hernández into reuniting Los Brujos, and Gilly was able to book the band for some gigs at a club called El Mocambo, but it wasn't anything permanent.

If Lonnie brought up the subject of money, his dad would tell him not to worry about it and to just focus on school. What he didn't realize was that with all the chores Lonnie had to do, he had little time left for his studies. His dad expected him to do all the housework, just like he had done with his wife.

A week after Lonnie's grandparents' surprise visit, a case worker from Child Protective Services showed up at their house. The woman introduced herself as Peggy Fontaine, but Lonnie's dad made her produce her ID before letting her in.

The second she entered the house, Ms. Fontaine's eyes darted around. Luckily, Lonnie had cleaned house the day before. When she shook his hand, she reeled him in and sniffed his hair, while giving his clothes a subtle glance.

They sat in the living room, which was seldom used except for company. Ms. Fontaine was pleasant, but Lonnie knew this wasn't a social call. She had come to see if there was any truth to his grandpa's allegations that his dad was doing a poor job raising him. She asked Lonnie's dad how they were adjusting.

"It's hard, as you can imagine, but we're doing the best we can," he said.

Ms. Fontaine asked him if he was working, and he told her about Los Brujos and their gigs at El Mocambo.

"Plus, I still got my unemployment checks coming in," he said. "I'm also following up on some job leads, and I oughta be hearing something pretty soon."

"Where does Lonnie stay when you perform with your band?" Ms. Fontaine asked.

"Well, you know, he's thirteen, and he's pretty responsible for his age. Lonnie does a lot of the cleaning and cooking around here, so he knows how to take care of himself."

A lot of the cleaning and cooking? Lonnie did all of it, but he didn't tell the case worker that.

"Just to make sure he's okay, I have our neighbor, Mrs. Escamilla, check in on him from time to time. Her daughter Carmen used to babysit Lonnie when he was little. Usually, though, he spends the evenings doing his homework." He turned to his son. "Right, buddy?"

"Where do you do your homework, Lonnie?" Ms. Fontaine wanted to know.

"In my room."

"May I see it, please?"

"Sure."

Whenever his mom went inside his room, Lonnie would panic because she would see that he had lied about having cleaned it. But Ms. Fontaine was met by a neatly organized room, with everything in its place. Again, her eyes roved around, making Lonnie nervous because his walls were covered with horror movie posters. She also directed her attention to his DVD rack.

"I see you like monster movies," she said.

"He's like any boy his age," Lonnie's dad interjected. "You know how they love all that stuff."

Lonnie's interest in horror films didn't appear to bother Ms. Fontaine because she didn't say anything else about it.

"How are you doing in school, Lonnie?" she asked.

Again, his dad answered for him. "I ain't gonna lie to you, Miss. Lonnie's grades ain't what they should be, but you can understand that, with his mom passing and everything. But we're working on it."

"What's your favorite subject?" she asked.

"Texas history," Lonnie said. "I've got this really cool teacher who likes to dress up in costumes when he teaches."

"When I was in school, I couldn't stand any of my teachers," his dad told her. "I had this one teacher. Her name was—"

"Do you have many friends at school?" Ms. Fontaine broke in. "Do you get along with your classmates?"

"Yeah, I've got lots of friends," Lonnie said. "Both guys and girls. And they've all been really supportive."

"That's good." Ms. Fontaine lifted the bed cover and peeked at the sheets. "May I see your kitchen?" she asked Lonnie's dad.

"You bet," he said and led the way.

Without asking for permission, Ms. Fontaine opened the pantry and looked inside. Next, she checked the refrigerator and the freezer. Lonnie wasn't worried. They had plenty of groceries. If she was concerned about all the beer in the fridge, she didn't mention it.

After a few minutes, she said, "Thank you for showing me around. Everything looks fine. I apologize for the intrusion."

"Hey, you're welcome to come by any time," Lonnie's dad said. "We ain't got nothing to hide. Oh, and you tell that father-in-law of mine to keep his nose out of our business and let me and Lonnie get on with our lives."

Lonnie wished his dad hadn't ended their visit on a sour note, but it didn't seem to faze Ms. Fontaine. She got in her car and drove off.

Hopefully, that was the last time they would have to deal with CPS.

CHAPTER FOURTEEN

LONNIE'S FIRST REPORT CARD OF THE YEAR came out. He received an F in math, an F in science, and a C in Progressive Reading. On the positive side, he did get an A in P.E., but Coach Rizzo gave everyone an A if they had perfect attendance. Lonnie had missed a few days of school, but Coach understood and let those days slide. Lonnie also got an A in art, but Ms. Tedesco, like Coach Rizzo, was an easy grader.

The grade he was most proud of was the B plus he made in Texas history. Lonnie thought he could have gotten an A, and maybe next time he would.

Mr. Bigelow pulled him out of class once again to see how he was doing. Lonnie assured him that he was fine and was trying to move on to the next chapter in his life.

Lonnie found himself spending less time with Axel. They didn't share classes, and the only time they saw each other was at lunch. Even then, they didn't always sit together. They were traveling in different paths. Axel was an honors student, and it had been ingrained in him since birth that he was going to go to college. Lonnie could only hope to graduate from high school. Axel's parents were actively involved in their children's lives, whether at school, at church or at home. Lonnie's mother was dead, and his dad was dead drunk most of the time.

Lonnie tried hanging out with some of the other guys—Noe, Fernando and Bobby—but they were on the Wyatt Wranglers football team, and they mostly talked about their games. He wished he could join the team, but with the grades he was making, the coaches wouldn't have allowed him to be the water boy.

On the way to first period, the hallway traffic suddenly stopped. Kids were pointing and laughing, but Lonnie couldn't see what was causing the commotion. When he finally squeezed through the crowds, he saw Mr. Arrington in his strangest getup yet. He had on a long dress, a bonnet and a dark wig.

"Who are you supposed to be, Mr. Arrington?" Lonnie asked.

"My dear young man," he replied in a falsetto voice. "I am not Mr. Arrington. My name is Jane Long."

"Who's Jane Long?"

Without breaking character, Mr. Arrington said, "Please take your seat inside the school house, Lon Chaney. You shall learn my story shortly."

Lonnie entered the classroom and saw Yvette sitting at her desk, searching through her purse. Since she was alone, he decided to talk to her.

"Mr. Arrington sure looks funny, doesn't he?" Lonnie said.

Yvette jumped, and he realized he had startled her. "Oh, hi, Lonnie. Yeah, he does look pretty funny. He's supposed to be Jane Long, whoever that is." She pulled a pen out of her purse and scribbled circles on a sheet of paper to see if it worked.

"Do you know who Mr. Arrington reminds me of?" Lonnie asked. "Our fourth-grade teacher, Mr. Treviño."

"You're right. Mr. Treviño was cool, just like Mr. Arrington."

"I ran into him at the grocery store not too long ago," Lonnie said.

"Really? Is he still teaching at Lamar?"

"Yep. Same school, same room," Lonnie said, quoting Mr. Treviño.

"I'd love to go back sometime to see—"

The bell sounded.

"We'll talk later," he told her and sat down.

Mr. Arrington entered the classroom. In a high voice, he said, "Good morning, children. My name is Jane Long. Some people know me as the Mother of Texas."

The class erupted into cheers and applause.

In first-person narrative, Mr. Arrington recounted Jane Long's story. As ridiculous as the teacher looked in his dress and wig, Lonnie was nevertheless drawn back to the early 1800s, when Jane Long, one of the first Anglo females to settle in Texas, endured the hardships of winter at Bolivar Point. This is where she gave birth to her third child, while waiting for her husband to return from Mexico, not realizing he had been killed there.

Having teachers like Mr. Treviño and Mr. Arrington made Lonnie think that if he didn't grow up to become a horror film actor, he might like to go into teaching.

When the bell rang, he waited for Yvette to get up so they could leave together. They didn't share second period, but he thought that as long as they were both headed in the same direction, he could escort her to her next class.

No such luck. Megan Patterson and Lisa Yarbrough met her outside the door, automatically positioning themselves, one on each side of her, like a pair of bookends, and the three of them walked down the hallway together.

During math class, Mrs. Ridley called Lonnie to her desk. He dreaded having to hear what she had to say. She went over his grades with him. Then she handed him a permission form for his dad to sign and told him he needed to begin attending after-school tutoring if he expected to pass the semester. Lonnie realized he needed help with math, but with so much housework to do, plus homework, he didn't know how he was going to fit tutoring into his schedule.

Because he had also failed science, he expected to receive the same lecture and permission form from Mr. Malone. His science teacher didn't mention anything about tutoring, and Lonnie got the feeling that as old and decrepit as he was, Mr. Malone didn't want to stay after school any later than he had to.

In Progressive Reading, Ms. Kowalski placed Lonnie in a small reading group with Herman Gilmore, the dimwit formerly known as Slurpee, and some other low readers. They were given soft cover books to read from a reading program called Breakthrough Books. Lonnie didn't think anything could be more boring than *The Dumfrees Move In*, but Breakthrough Books proved him wrong. While Ms. Kowalski had the flunkies take turns reading aloud, Lonnie made a mental list of the items he had to pick up when he went grocery shopping. His dad had turned that responsibility over to him as well, saying that since Lonnie was doing all the cooking, he had a better idea of what to buy.

After Progressive Reading, Lonnie had art class, which he always found enjoyable. Ms. Tedesco had been teaching the principles of perspective drawing, and for a class assignment, she had her students draw pictures of landscapes. The first thing that popped into Lonnie's mind was Catfish Creek, so he sketched that. He also added a silhouette of Moses splashing in the water. When Ms. Tedesco asked him about the figure in his drawing, Lonnie told her that his name was Moses. She suggested that he should reread his Bible stories because Moses had been rescued from the water as a baby, not as an adult.

Lonnie's last class was P.E. Most of the time, they didn't work on anything specific. Coach Rizzo simply let his students shoot baskets or hang out on the blacktop while he talked on his phone.

In the other P.E. periods, students were required to bathe before going to their next class, but since P.E was Lonnie's last class of the day, he had the option of skipping the shower. Usually he waited until the following morning to bathe, but he had begun to shower at school because it was one less thing he had to do at home.

His mother would have been pleasantly surprised by his interest in his personal hygiene. She used to harp on him constantly about his body odor.

Looking back at all the grief and heartaches he had caused her, Lonnie wished he had been a better son. He should've made better grades. He should've been more truthful. He should've cleaned his room when she told him. He had learned how to cook, how to wash, how to iron and how to clean house. He could've helped her with all those things. Sadly, the should'ves and could'ves had arrived too late to do any good.

Thoughts about his mom brought a painful feeling to his chest, and Lonnie's eyes grew misty. Not wanting anyone to see him cry, he cut through the breezeway that separates the gym from the main campus and hurried toward the blacktop behind the school. He had planned to take the back streets home because they were less congested with parents and students. But just as he reached the teachers' parking lot, he ran into Jo Marie, who was standing next to the fence with Patricia, Carolyn and Regina.

Noticing the tears in his eyes, Jo Marie asked, "Lonnie, are you all right?"

Oh, man! That's all I need. A bunch of girls to see me cry.

He wiped his eyes and sniffled. "Yeah, I'm okay."

"Are you sure?"

At that moment, Lonnie lost it. All the emotions he had kept pent up for the past several weeks gushed out, like water from a busted dam, and he began to bawl uncontrollably.

Jo Marie took him in her arms. He placed his face on her shoulder and cried with more anguish than he'd done since learning that his mom had died. He couldn't stop. The tears kept coming. She rocked him tenderly, like a mother comforting her baby.

Out of the corner of his eye, Lonnie saw Jo Marie nudge her head toward the girls. She mouthed something he didn't hear, but he figured she had told them to go on without her.

They held onto each other a little longer. Finally, Lonnie dried his eyes with his shirt sleeve. "I'm sorry, Jo Marie. This is so embarrassing."

"Don't be embarrassed," she said. "We're friends, aren't we?"

"It's just that I've never cried like this in front of a girl."

"Would it have been better if I was a boy?"

Lonnie chuckled. "I guess not."

She led him to a live oak tree on the other end of the parking lot, where they could talk privately.

"I won't say that I know what you're going through," Jo Marie said, "because I've never lost someone close. But I know it's got to be tough trying to adjust to life without your mom."

"It's not just that," Lonnie said, then paused when he felt another round of tears about to flood out. Turning away, he broke off a piece of bark from the tree and pretended to study it. "Have you ever seen the movie, *Dr. Jekyll and Mr. Hyde*?"

"No, but I'm familiar with the story. Why?"

"Well, I was sort of like Dr. Jekyll with my mom," he said. "That's the side of me I wanted her to see. You know, the good side. But there's also the Mr. Hyde part of me, the bad side that I kept hidden from her." Lonnie didn't know why he was opening up to Jo Marie. She didn't exactly top his list of favorite people. Maybe it was because she was religious. Or maybe he just needed to talk things out with someone.

Jo Marie looked puzzled. "What do you mean?"

He threw down the piece of bark and looked around to make sure no one could hear. "I used to lie to my mom all the time," he admitted. "About everything. At first, it was just small stuff. She'd ask me if I'd cleaned my room, and I'd tell her that I had when I really hadn't. If she asked me how I was doing in school, I'd say fine, even though I was flunking all my classes."

"Well, that hardly makes you a bad person," Jo Marie said, dismissing his concern. "I don't tell my parents everything, either."

"It gets worse," he said. "My mom used to make me go to your church every Sunday. But instead listening to your dad preach, I'd sneak out the back door to hang out at Catfish Creek until church was over."

Jo Marie shrugged. "So you don't like to hear my dad preach. You're probably not the only one."

Her response took him aback. He expected her to say something critical or quote a Bible verse about God's judgment. But since she didn't, he continued. "The thing is, I was lying to my mom. Just like I used to lie to her whenever I wanted to get out of the house. I'd tell her I was going to Axel's, but instead, I'd go to the paper company or to Catfish Creek or some other place."

Jo Marie had already heard about the break-in at the warehouse, but Lonnie told her everything, including the part where he confessed to his mom about his involvement and how she reacted when she found out.

"Now I have to live every day, knowing that the last thing my mom remembered about me was that I was a liar. The night she died, she told me she couldn't trust me anymore. She said that everything that came out of my mouth was a lie. She..." He lowered his head and shuddered with tears.

"No, Lonnie, you're wrong," Jo Marie said. "Look at me." She took his face in her hands. "Look at me! Your mom's last thoughts about you weren't that you were a liar. Her last thoughts were that you finally told her the truth. That's what she remembered. You have to believe that. You just have to!" She wrapped her arms around him again. "I can't imagine how hard it's been for you to live with all that guilt. But please know that your mom didn't think bad of you. She never stopped loving you. She forgave you, just like God has forgiven you. Promise me you'll focus on that. You're not Dr. Jekyll or Mr. Hyde.

You're a boy who lost his mother, and that's hard enough to deal with. You don't need a guilt trip eating you up."

Of all the people in the world, Jo Marie was the last person Lonnie thought he would go to for comfort, but he was glad he did. He held her a little longer before pulling away, feeling drained and exhausted, yet somehow cleansed, as if all his sorrows had been washed away.

"Thank you, Jo Marie," he said softly.

She wiped away her tears. "Hey, that's what friends are for, right? Now come on. I need someone to walk me home."

CHAPTER FIFTEEN

LONNIE'S HOUSE WAS UNUSUALLY QUIET when he arrived. The TV wasn't on, and his dad wasn't asleep on the couch. The Suburban was parked in the driveway, so Lonnie knew he was home.

"Dad?"

No answer.

"Dad, I'm home."

Still nothing.

He peeked in his dad's bedroom. It was empty. He checked the study. The same. He wasn't in the bathroom, either.

When Lonnie looked in the kitchen, he recoiled in horror. He found his dad slumped in a chair, eyes closed, with a gun dangling in his hand. The gun holster and three beer cans sat on top of the breakfast table.

"DAD!"

He opened his eyes slowly. "Oh, hey, buddy. You home already?"

"Dad, give me the gun," Lonnie said.

"What?"

Lonnie inched closer toward him with his hand outstretched. "Dad, please. Just give me the gun."

He stared at it and made a face. "Whoa, what did you think I was gonna do, buddy?" He slipped the gun back in its holster. "I know I ain't the smartest guy in the world, but I ain't crazy."

"What are you doing with Mom's gun?" Lonnie asked, still feeling spooked.

His dad picked up a can and finished the rest of the beer. "I was trying to figure out where I could get some money," he said. "Then I got an idea. I'm gonna take your mom's gun to a pawn shop to see what they'll give me for it. I was looking it over, and I guess I must've dozed off."

With a silent sigh of relief, Lonnie pulled out a chair and sat down. As a precaution, he moved the gun away from his dad. "Have you heard anything from those places where you applied?"

His dad shook his head. "Nobody's hiring right now. I mean nobody. And when I do get a bite, there's always that question on the application that asks, 'Why did you leave your last job?' I can't lie about it. They're gonna check. Or they'll ask, 'Have you ever been convicted of a crime?' What am I supposed to say? Yeah, but I promise I won't do it again?"

"Somebody has to hire you eventually," Lonnie said, trying to sound optimistic.

"Like who?" His dad picked up an empty beer can and crushed it like an accordion. "I don't know how to do nothing, except drive a truck. But with a DWI conviction on my record, nobody's gonna give me a job doing that."

Changing the subject, Lonnie asked, "How much do you think you can get for Mom's gun?"

"Couple of hundred, maybe. But it's worth a lot more." His dad folded his arms on the table and gave Lonnie a despairing look. "I'm gonna be honest with you, buddy. Things ain't going too good right now. I thought we'd have some money left over from your mom's insurance policy, but the cost of the funeral took it all. I was able to pay most of last month's bills, but I don't know how long I can keep doing it."

This was the first time his dad had been open about their money problems. Lonnie knew it had been gnawing at him, but up until now, he hadn't wanted to worry him with it. Still, he didn't have anyone else he could confide in. His dad was too proud to ask his parents for help. And he wasn't about to give his father-in-law any reason to suspect he was struggling financially.

"Maybe we could have a yard sale," Lonnie suggested. "We have a lot of stuff we don't need that we can get rid of."

"Yeah, I thought about that. And I hate to do it, but I'm gonna have to pawn some of your mom's jewelry. Also, I'm gonna turn in my Suburban 'cause I can't afford to make the payments on it. I'll drive your mom's Impala. I know her car's old, but it's paid for."

"Dad, we're not in danger of going homeless, are we?" Lonnie asked, thinking about Moses.

"Homeless? 'Course not. Don't think like that, buddy. We're just going through a rough time, that's all. But like you said, somebody's gotta hire me eventually."

As long as his dad was discussing finances, Lonnie felt he needed to add something. He picked up the crushed beer can and said, "Maybe you shouldn't drink so much. Beer costs a lot of money, and we really can't afford it."

"Yeah, I know." His dad tossed the beer cans in the trash. Then he grabbed the gun and holster. "Get started on your homework, and I'll find something for us to eat."

"You're fixing dinner?" Lonnie asked.

"You think your old man don't know how to cook? I'm gonna make my specialty, *papas con huevo* with cheese and onions. Now go on. I'll call you when it's ready."

This was an unexpected surprise. Lonnie's dad had never offered to cook dinner before. Maybe he'd had a change of heart after seeing his son's report card, and he realized Lonnie couldn't keep up with all the chores and school work without help.

In his room, Lonnie opened his math book. They had been studying percentages, and Mrs. Ridley had assigned fifteen word problems for homework.

Lonnie read the first one. He tried to think back to how Mrs. Ridley had explained the process for solving this type of word problem, but he drew a blank, just like he had done in class. Mrs. Ridley was a soft talker, so it was easy for him to tune out whenever she demonstrated how to do the work. He jotted down a few calculations, made some guesses and answered the problem.

Forty minutes later, he completed his work. He didn't know if the answers were correct, but at least he was done with that assignment. He was about to get started on his science homework when his dad called him.

The table was set with forks, paper towels and two steaming dishes of fried potatoes, mixed with scrambled eggs, cheese and onions. In the middle of the table a folded kitchen towel kept the flour tortillas inside it warm.

"Smells good," Lonnie said.

His dad placed two iced tea glasses on the table. "And it tastes even better."

Lonnie wondered if his dad was planning to take over the cooking duties, but he didn't ask.

While they ate, his dad began to complain about not being able to find a job. "It's so frustrating, you know? Everywhere I go, the answer is no, no, no. It really makes me mad."

Cracking a smile, Lonnie said, "We all go a little mad sometimes. What movie does that line come from?"

His dad stared at him curiously. Then his face brightened. "*Psycho*. That's what Norman Bates said to Marion Crane."

"Pretty good, Dad, but that was easy. Let's see if you know this one. In the movie, *The Day the Earth Stood Still*, what were Klaatu's instructions to Gort?"

"Wait. Don't tell me. I know this." His dad scratched his chin with his fork. "Klaatu barada nikto."

"That's right. Now you give me one."

His dad wiped his mouth with his paper towel. "Okay, in the *Friday the 13th* movies, what kind of mask does Jason wear?"

"Aw, come on, Dad. That's too easy. Give me something harder."

"Then go ahead and tell me, smart guy. What kind of mask does Jason wear?"

"A hockey mask," Lonnie replied with a roll of his eyes. "Everybody knows that."

"Wrong, buddy. Jason didn't start wearing the hockey mask till *Friday the 13th* Part 3. In Part 2, he wore a sack with a hole in it, and in Part 1, he didn't wear a mask."

"You're gonna need a bigger boat," Lonnie quoted.

"*Jaws*," his dad answered right away. Then he asked, "What was the name of the clown in the movie *It*?"

"Pennywise," Lonnie said, raising his arms in victory.

It had been months since they had played horror movie trivia. Lonnie's mom never understood any of the references, so she usually ignored them.

In a thick accent, Lonnie's dad said, "Listen to them, the children of the night. What sweet music they make. Who am I?"

Pretending to wrap a cape around his face, Lonnie answered in a similar accent, "Dracula."

"I like Dracula," his dad said. "But he's a real pain in the neck."

"You know, he used to be an artist," Lonnie joked. "He loved to draw blood."

"Yeah, but he sucked at it," his dad said, and they both laughed for the first time since before Lonnie's mother passed away.

CHAPTER SIXTEEN

Saturday morning, Lonnie and his dad held a yard sale in front of their house. Ms. Tedesco had given Lonnie permission to make two YARD SALE signs in art class. He stapled them to wooden stakes and stuck them into the ground near the sidewalk. Lonnie had found the stakes at a construction site and had taken them home because they reminded him of the ones movie vampires were killed with.

His dad borrowed two folding tables from Gilly. He used them to display some of the smaller items they were selling. He also tied a rope between two trees where he hung up clothes, mostly his wife's, but also some of Lonnie's that he had outgrown.

Lonnie contributed his action figures, board games, a soccer ball, a baseball bat and ball, comic books and magazines. He also brought out his entire DVD collection to sell, which he hated to do, but they needed every cent they could get.

They hadn't planned to start the sale until eight o'clock, but at seven-thirty, while they were setting up, two cars pulled up in front of their house. A man and a woman stepped out of the first car, and three ladies, friends of the couple, slid out of the car behind them.

The women took their time looking over each item, but the man zeroed in on Lonnie's box of DVDs. As he read through the titles, his eyes widened.

"How much?" he asked Lonnie.

"Uh, they're two dollars each." Lonnie said. He had paid a lot more for the DVDs, but his dad had told him that people were more likely to buy their merchandise if they sold it at a cheap price.

"What do you want for the whole box?" the man asked.

It hadn't occurred to Lonnie that someone would want to buy all of them. There were ninety-two DVDs in the box. Times two dollars each would make the price a hundred and eighty-four dollars. But since the man was willing to buy the whole collection, Lonnie decided to give him a discount. "I'll take a hundred and seventy-five dollars for them," he said.

The man pulled out a wad of bills from his pocket and ran his fingers through them. "Tell you what, sonny. I'll give you a hundred bucks for the whole thing. What do you say?"

"A hundred bucks?" Lonnie was insulted by the offer. "Mister, these DVDs are worth a lot more than that." He fished out *Return to Darkness*. "I paid almost twenty dollars for this one."

His dad heard their conversation and came over. "What's going on?"

"Dad, he says he wants to buy all my DVDs, but he only wants to give me a hundred bucks for them."

The man grabbed a handful of DVDs and spread them apart in his hands, like playing cards. "Sure, you've got a few good ones in the bunch. But most of them, like *Attack of the Sewer Rats* and *A Howl in the Night,* ain't worth more than four bits apiece."

"Let me talk to my son," Lonnie's dad told him. "You go ahead and look around. See if there's anything else you wanna buy."

He took Lonnie aside, away from the shoppers. "Listen, buddy. Don't let that guy rattle you. This is a strategy yard sale hunters use. They make you a low offer and hope they can buy it at that price, but they're usually willing to pay more. I guarantee you that guy runs a booth in a flea market or has a used DVD store, where he'll sell your movies for a lot more."

"What should I tell him?" Lonnie asked.

"Say that you'll take a hundred and fifty."

"And what if he says no?"

"Then you negotiate with him."

One of the ladies held up a mirror and called Lonnie's dad over. Lonnie took a deep breath and walked up to the man.

"How about a hundred and fifty dollars?" he asked.

The man furrowed his brows. "I'll go as high as a hundred and thirty, but that's it."

"Make it a hundred and forty and you've got yourself a deal," Lonnie said, trying to keep his voice from quaking.

"One forty? That's still a lot of money."

"It's only ten dollars more than what you offered me. What do you say?"

"You drive a hard bargain, sonny, but . . . okay, one forty it is." The man pulled the wad of bills from his pocket again and counted out the money.

It bugged Lonnie to have to sell his DVDs for almost nothing, but at least they now had a hundred and forty dollars more than what they started out with.

The ladies bought a rocking chair, the mirror one of them had asked about, a still-life flower painting, two dresses and a small bookcase.

≈ ≈ ≈

It wasn't eight o'clock yet, but already they had made a little over two hundred dollars. At this rate, Lonnie thought they would have a pile of money by the end of the day.

Customers continued to arrive. Soon, they had a yard full of people, some buying, but many more just looking around.

At a quarter till nine, Lonnie's grandparents Salinas showed up.

"Looks like you still haven't found a job yet," Lonnie's grandpa told his son-in-law.

"Why do you say that?"

"Because if you had, you wouldn't need to have a yard sale."

"I'm just getting rid of some old stuff. Nothing wrong with that."

"Well, have you?"

"Have I what?"

"Have you found a job?"

Lonnie's dad glared at him. "I'm telling you again, Arthur. That's none of your business. You wanna buy something, fine, but—"

"Arthur!" Lonnie's grandma shrieked. She rushed over, holding a glass bowl. "Do you see what Richard's selling?"

"It's a punch bowl," Lonnie's dad said. "So what?"

"No, it's not," she said, flabbergasted. "This is Waterford crystal. We gave it to you and Becky for a wedding present."

"Okay, so it was a wedding present. But we ain't married no more."

Lonnie's grandma cradled the bowl in her arms, as if she was holding a baby. "I can't believe you would sell it for fifteen dollars."

"You think that's too much?" Lonnie's dad asked.

She blinked in disbelief. "Richard, we paid almost five hundred dollars for this bowl."

"How much do you think I should ask for it then? A hundred?"

"I don't want you to sell it at all," she said. "If you can't appreciate something this valuable, I want it back."

"You can't have it back. But I'll sell it to you, if you wanna buy it. For fifteen bucks, like the sticker on the bowl says."

"Look, Richard," Lonnie's grandpa started.

"No, you look! I'm tired of you showing up at my house without calling first."

"We have a right to see Lonnie. You can't stop us from seeing our grandson."

"I ain't saying you can't see him. I just want you to call to let me know you're coming."

"Why? Are you hiding something?"

"No, it's just good manners."

Lonnie's grandpa sneered at him. "And what if we don't call?"

"Then maybe as soon as you show up, me and Lonnie will suddenly have a bunch of errands to run."

"We only came to invite Lonnie to join us for breakfast," Lonnie's grandma said, still holding the crystal bowl tightly against her body. Turning to her grandson, she asked, "How have you been, *mijo*?"

"Real good, Grandma."

"You look skinny. Are you getting enough to eat?"

"I'm eating fine."

"*Hmmph*. Junk food," Lonnie's grandpa said.

"No, really. We hardly ever eat out," Lonnie told him. "Me and my dad cook just about every night." Lonnie felt he needed to include his dad, even though he had only prepared dinner once.

"We came to pick you up to take you to Denny's," his grandpa said.

"I can't," Lonnie said. "I need to help my dad with the yard sale. Besides, I've already eaten. But thanks anyway."

A woman with a little boy called Lonnie's dad over because she wanted to pay for three action figures and a pair of wall sconces.

"I'd better use the bathroom before we leave," Lonnie's grandpa said. He gave his wife an eye signal. "You probably need to go too, don't you?"

"What? Oh, yes. I'd better go." She handed Lonnie the crystal bowl. "Don't drop it, and don't let anyone buy it."

While Lonnie's dad was distracted with customers, his in-laws entered the house through the kitchen door.

They both might have had sudden urges to pee, but Lonnie doubted it. More than likely, they had gone inside to snoop around. Luckily, the house was spotless.

A few minutes later, his grandparents walked out, and his grandma took the crystal bowl from Lonnie. "Are you sure you don't want to join us for breakfast?"

"Yeah, I'm sure, Grandma. But thanks for inviting me."

As they started up the walkway Lonnie's dad hollered at them, "Hey! You didn't pay for that bowl."

His mother-in-law scowled at him.

"Fifteen bucks," Lonnie's dad said, holding out his hand.

Lonnie's grandpa drew his wallet from his back pocket, took out a ten and a five and slapped them in his son-in-law's hand. "You happy now?"

"I appreciate your business, Arthur. Y'all have a good day."

On the way to their car, Lonnie's grandma's heel got caught in a crack on the sidewalk, and she stumbled. Her husband grabbed her by the arm, but as he did, she let go of the crystal bowl and it fell, shattering in pieces.

"Sweet," Lonnie's dad said, grinning.

At five-thirty, they shut down the yard sale. After putting away everything that didn't sell, they sat on the porch to relax — Lonnie with a Coke and his dad with a beer. Lonnie knew his dad would never stop drinking, but he was glad that he was making a stronger effort to curtail his habit.

They made $476 from the sale. Earlier in the week, Lonnie's dad pawned his wife's gun, as well as their wedding rings, plus a couple of other rings and a necklace. When they added that money to what they had made from the yard sale, Lonnie thought they were in great shape, financially.

He sat back in a lawn chair and enjoyed the cool October air. The trees had begun to turn colors, and some of them had started to lose their leaves. By the end of November, his dad would have him raking them up.

Lonnie had no way of knowing that he would never again rake a single leaf from their yard.

CHAPTER SEVENTEEN

DETECTIVE PAUL CAMPBELL from the Marsville Homicide Division called Lonnie's dad to notify him that Kevin Williams, the man who murdered his wife, had been killed by his cellmate. They had gotten into an argument, and the cellmate slammed Kevin Williams' head against the wall, causing him to die from blunt force trauma.

"Well, at least we won't have to deal with a trial and go through the whole thing again," Lonnie's dad mused. "I guess that's what you call poetic justice."

Justice? Lonnie hadn't been looking forward to the trial, but he wanted to stare at Kevin Williams' eyes when the prosecutors took him apart. He wanted to hear him say he was sorry for what he had done and apologize to them. That wouldn't happen now. Kevin Williams was dead, but not for the crime he had committed. As far as Lonnie was concerned, his death wasn't punishment enough.

They celebrated Thanksgiving in Abilene, at Lonnie's grandparents Rodríguez's house, the first time they had done so. Ever since his dad stormed out, years ago, and moved to Marsville, his relationship with his parents had been strained.

If any ill feelings existed between them, no one showed it. Lonnie's grandparents graciously welcomed them into their home. Already, the house was filled with relatives, most of whom Lonnie had never seen before.

The air inside was rich with delicious aromas of meats, vegetables, breads and desserts. Every inch of counter space in the kitchen had been taken up with covered dishes. Pots warmed on the stove, and a turkey heated in the oven.

After greeting everyone, Lonnie and his dad joined a group of family members in the den to watch a football game between the Detroit Lions and the Green Bay Packers.

Lonnie looked out the sliding glass door and saw his cousin Enrique tossing a football with another cousin, Julián, in the back yard, so he went outside.

The moment he stepped onto the porch, Enrique threw the ball to him in a fast, tight spiral. "Catch it, Lonnie!"

Though taken by surprise, Lonnie raised his hands and caught the ball with ease. He threw it to Julián, who dropped it, but quickly picked it up and flung it to Enrique.

They continued playing catch, until a teen-aged girl appeared on the porch.

"Whoa, who's that babe?" Lonnie asked Julián

"Put your tongue back in your mouth, *primo*," he said. "That's Rita. She's your cousin."

"My cousin?" Lonnie said, embarrassed.

Julián laughed. "That's the thing about living in Abilene, *primo*. The Rodríguezes are spread all over town, so you've got to be real careful who you hit on, 'cause she could turn out to be a relative. Come on, I'll introduce you to her."

It dawned on Lonnie that Rita was his aunt Lydia's daughter. He hadn't seen her since they were little kids.

"Rita, say hi to Lon Chaney, your *primo* from Marsville," Julián said.

She giggled. "Lon Chaney? Are you serious? Who are your brothers? Boris Karloff and Bela Lugosi?"

"Just call me Lonnie," he said.

"Lonnie?" Rita gave a start of surprise. "Oh, my *gatos*! You're Tío Richard's son, right? The one who's mom . . ." She reached up and hugged him. "I'm sorry I didn't recognize you. It's been a long time."

"I guess you weren't at the funeral then?"

"No, my mom couldn't take off from work. How are you doing? I mean, with everything that's happened?"

"I have my good days and bad days," Lonnie said with a shrug.

"How long are you going to be in Abilene?"

"Until Sunday, I think. We're staying here with my grandparents."

"Cool," Enrique said. "Maybe we can do some stuff while you're in town."

"What stuff?" Julián asked. "There's nothing to do in Abilene, except to watch the tumbleweeds roll by."

"Don't listen to him," Rita said. "There are lots of things to do."

"Name one," Julián said.

"Well, there's the Mall of Abilene. We can go there."

"Trust me, *primo*," Julián said. "Watching the tumbleweeds roll by is more exciting than hanging out at the Mall of Abilene."

"What grade are you in?" Rita asked.

Lonnie held up seven fingers. "Seventh."

"Me, too. So are Henry K and Julián."

"Who's Henry K?" Lonnie asked.

"That's what we call Enrique," Rita said. "It's an old joke. When he was in the first grade, he had this teacher . . . what was her name?"

"Mrs. Culpepper," Enrique answered with a smile, knowing what was coming next.

"That's right. Anyway, Mrs. Culpepper was a southern-belle type with a thick *suthen* accent. Whenever she said Enrique's name, it came out as En-ree-kay, and I thought she was calling him Henry K. So the name stuck, and now he's Henry K."

"Do you guys spend a lot of time together?" Lonnie asked, thinking about how much fun it would be to hang out with them.

"I'd say so," Rita replied, looking at her cousins for confirmation. "The three of us go to Red Adair Middle School. Henry K's on the football team."

"Yeah, he told me. Do you play football, too?" Lonnie asked Julián.

"Are you kidding?" Henry K said. "Rita plays better football than him. Watch. Rita, go long."

She took off running, her pony tail bobbing on her back. Henry K threw a bomb, high in the air. Rita looked up over her right shoulder, reached for the ball and brought it in. Lonnie gawked in amazement at how athletic she was. He didn't know if he could have caught that pass.

"Go for it, Henry K!" Rita shouted, throwing the ball back to him. He caught it, then tossed it to Lonnie.

The four of them took a corner of the yard and threw passes to each other. Henry K was right about Julián, though. Rita was a much better player than he was. Half the time, he dropped the ball.

"You know, if you lived here, you could go to school with us," Rita told Lonnie after a while.

Henry K cracked a smile. "Yeah, and if you're real lucky, you could have Mr. Tovar for math. Hey, you kids . . . " he started, then the three of them chimed in together, "Get off da lockers!" and hooted with laughter.

"What does that mean?" Lonnie asked.

Rita caught her breath. "Nothing. It's just something stupid we say."

"No, it's something stupid Mr. Tovar says," Henry K said. "We just repeat it."

"I think it'd be cool going to school with you guys," Lonnie told them.

"Believe me, *primo*," Julián said. "You do not want to live in Abilene. Man, I'd do anything to move out of here."

"I don't know about that. I kind of like Abilene," Lonnie said, although moving here was unlikely. His dad had been estranged from his family for years. The only reason they were in town was because they had nowhere else to celebrate Thanksgiving.

Tía Lydia came out to announce that lunch was ready. After they washed up, Lonnie and his cousins joined the rest of the family around the table, and everyone held hands.

"We have so much for which to be thankful today," Lonnie's grandpa Rodríguez said, standing at the head of the table. "Our country, our health and our family. We're also grateful that Richard and Lonnie could be with us, especially after their loss."

Rita, who was standing next to Lonnie, squeezed his hand.

"Before we eat, is there anyone who would like to lead us in a word of prayer?" Lonnie's grandpa asked.

Everyone looked around, but no one offered. Finally Lonnie's dad said, "Lonnie knows how to pray. He goes to church."

Lonnie stared at him, aghast. "Dad, I . . . "

"All right! Go for it, Lonnie," Henry K said.

"Lonnie! Lonnie! Lonnie!" he and Julián and Rita chanted.

Lonnie didn't know what to do. He had never prayed in public before, but all eyes were on him. He bowed his head and searched his mind for the right words. Everyone grew silent and bowed with him.

"God is great . . . " Lonnie started slowly. "God is good . . . " He paused, thinking how ridiculous it was to recite a baby prayer on Thanksgiving Day.

Rita, Henry K and Julián came to his rescue. They finished the prayer in unison. "Let us thank Him for our food." They ended it with, "Amen, Brother Ben. Shot a goose and killed a hen."

Lonnie's grandpa looked at them and said dryly, "Well, that was different."

In addition to turkey and dressing, ham, green beans, mashed potatoes, plus tamales, refried beans and Spanish rice were served, along with tortillas, rolls and cornbread. Some of the adults sat at the dining table, the little kids sat at the breakfast table and everyone else sat wherever they could find a place. Lonnie and his cousins took their food to the front porch and sat on the railing.

"I have an idea," Rita said. "Let's go to the show tomorrow. I've been dying to see that new movie, *Fatal Dreams*."

"You like horror movies?" Lonnie asked. He had seen the trailer for *Fatal Dreams*, and it looked scary.

"I love them," she said. "They always give me nightmares, but I watch them anyway."

"I saw that movie last week," Julián said. "It was terrible. The special effects were so lame. They didn't even show the demon until the last few minutes of the movie, and he looked like that little red devil on the potted meat can."

"Thanks for spoiling it for us, dum-dum," Rita said. "But I still want to see it."

"Me, too," Henry K said. "And on Saturday, we'll take Lonnie to Frontier Texas."

"What's that?" Lonnie asked.

"It's a museum with lots of cool stuff about the Old West."

"Or we could go to the zoo," Rita suggested.

Lonnie wished he could do all those things, but he knew he wouldn't be able to do any of them. His dad was running short on cash, and he had griped about how much money he had spent on gas to make the trip.

Nevertheless, Lonnie told his cousins, "I'll talk to my dad and see what he says."

After they had eaten, they gathered in the den with the other football fans to watch the game between the Dallas Cowboys and the New Orleans Saints.

During half-time, with Dallas leading 14 to 3, everyone got up to take a break. Lonnie went to the kitchen to get another slice of pecan pie and some more soda.

On the way back, he heard what sounded like an argument coming from one of the bedrooms. The door was ajar, so he stood outside and peeked in. His uncles, his aunt and his grandpa were gathered around his dad.

"But I don't need it," Lonnie's dad said, pushing Tío Daniel's hand away. "Really. Me and Lonnie are doing fine."

"*Ándale*, Richard, take it," Tío Daniel insisted, holding a wad of money in his hand. "We know you're going through a hard time right now, so Lydia, Rogelio, Armando and I chipped in two hundred dollars each to help you out."

"No, that's okay. I'm good. As a matter of fact, I just got a job. Starting Monday, I'll be working at a furniture store warehouse in Marsville."

"Really? Congratulations, man," Tío Daniel said. "That's awesome. I'm glad you finally found something. Still, it'll be awhile before you get paid, and the eight hundred dollars will tide you over until then."

"No, Daniel. I'm not gonna take your money," Lonnie's dad said. "But thanks for thinking about us."

He started to walk out of the bedroom when his father muttered, "If you'd gone to school like I told you, you wouldn't be in the bind you're in now."

Lonnie's dad wheeled around, his face filled with indignation. "So you're telling me that if I'd gone to college, Becky would still be alive? Is that what you're telling me, Pa?"

"No, but maybe if you'd gone to college and gotten a degree, Becky might not have had to work as a security guard to help make ends meet."

"She didn't have to work as a security guard. It's what she wanted to do. And I already had a job that paid me plenty of money."

"Working as a truck driver?" his father scoffed. "Come on, Richard. Who do you think you're kidding? You threw away a perfectly good opportunity for a real career. Everyone else went to school, and look at them now. Rogelio and Daniel are engineers, Armando's a high school principal and Lydia's an accountant. And what did you do? You became a truck driver, and you couldn't even make a go of that."

"Yeah, that's right. Go ahead. Let the whole world know that I'm the dumb one of the family!"

"I didn't say — "

"Yeah, you did. You think I've forgotten how you used to call me *burro* when I was little?"

"You were failing all your classes, Richard," his father said. "Instead of studying, you'd sit in your room for hours, playing your guitar. Do you think you deserved to be praised for that?"

"I didn't deserve to be called names! Lonnie's not doing too good in school, but I don't make fun of him for it." He pointed at his siblings. "That's why I don't wanna live in Abilene, Pa. 'Cause all you'll do is hold me up to them and say, 'Look, *burro*, that's what you could've become!'"

He stalked out of the bedroom. Seeing Lonnie standing in the hallway, he took him by the arm, making him spill his soda. "C'mon. We're going home."

"But I thought we were spending the weekend here."

"We're not spending another minute in this house. Get your jacket and let's get outta here."

When Rita saw them, she exclaimed, "Oh, my *gatos*! What happened?"

"I'll tell you later," Lonnie said and hugged her good-bye.

"Lonnie! Let's go!" his dad shouted, hurrying him out of the house.

As soon as they got in the car, he tore out of the driveway, sped down Ambler Street and headed toward Interstate 20.

"I shoulda known this wasn't gonna work," he said.

"What wouldn't work?" Lonnie asked.

"Coming here. I thought that as long as we were in town, I'd talk to my parents about me and you staying with them for a little while. You know, till things got better."

"You were considering moving us to Abilene?" Lonnie asked, astounded. "But what about your new job?"

"I ain't got no job. I only told my family that to get them off my back. The truth is, I ain't got nothing. No job, no prospects . . . and pretty soon, no house."

"Dad, what are you talking about?"

He sighed. "I ain't got the money for the rent, buddy. I hate to tell you this, but it looks like we're gonna have to move out of our house by the end of the month."

"We're moving? Where?"

"I don't know yet. I'll have to see what's out there."

"Wait a minute," Lonnie said. "If you knew you weren't going to be able to pay the rent, why didn't you take the eight hundred bucks they were trying to give you?"

"'Cause I wasn't gonna let my brothers and sister treat me like some charity case. I was about to talk to your grandpa about us living with them, till they showed up and started getting all uppity with me. Then . . . well, you saw what happened."

"So you were serious about us moving in with Grandma and Grandpa?"

"It don't matter 'cause it ain't gonna happen."

"But it could. I mean, if you were to go back and apologize . . . "

"Forget it. I ain't apologizing to nobody. Besides, you got your school."

"That's not a problem. I could easily transfer to Adair and go to school with Enrique and them."

Lonnie hated his school. He didn't have any close friends, except for Axel, and that relationship was going nowhere. Yvette was the only bright spot. But when he learned that she had been hanging out with Michael de Luna, the Wyatt Wrangler's quarterback, he knew he had no chance with her.

"As soon as we get back, I'm gonna start looking for a place for us to move to," his dad said.

"You mean to another house?"

"I don't know."

"An apartment?"

"Maybe. I don't know. Stop asking so many questions."

"Dad, you need to turn back," Lonnie said, fear now dawning inside him. "You have to apologize to Grandpa and tell him we need help. At least we'll have a place to live."

"Are you crazy? I ain't gonna do that."

"Dad, please. We can't go homeless."

"We're not gonna go homeless!"

"It's not fair! Just 'cause you don't want to work!" Lonnie snapped.

"Watch your mouth, buddy. It ain't that I don't wanna work. I'm trying my best to find a job, and as soon as I do, things are gonna get better."

"No, they're not!" Lonnie burst into tears. "Things are never going to get better 'cause you don't want them to. We could move in with Grandma and Grandpa right now, but you'd rather us go homeless than to do that."

"You don't know what you're talking about, so just keep your mouth shut, okay?"

"It's not fair! It's not fair!"

CHAPTER EIGHTEEN

"Hey, kid. C'mere."

Lonnie turned around and saw Moses perched on top of a boulder behind him. His legs were crossed, like a little kid in a reading circle. Lonnie started to run away, but for some reason, he didn't feel threatened by him.

"I ain't gonna hurt you," Moses said, motioning him over. "I just wanna talk to you."

Stepping away from the creek bank, Lonnie climbed up the hill and walked toward him, maintaining a safe distance, in case he decided to try something.

Moses stroked his long beard. "You got any money on you?"

"No, sir," Lonnie lied, thinking about the thirteen dollars in his wallet.

"Sir," Moses said quietly. "It's been a long time since somebody called me *sir*. What are you doing here, anyway?"

Lonnie shrugged. "Sometimes I come to Catfish Creek to get away from things."

"Yeah?" Moses brought down his legs. "What are you trying to get away from today?"

"Just some problems me and my dad are having."

"I know what you mean," he said. "Me and my old man didn't get along too good, either. Sit down, kid. Take a load off your dogs."

Something about the sound of his voice made Lonnie feel he could trust him, so he sat on a boulder across from him. "Do you live out here?" he asked.

Moses laughed. "Naw, I live at the Waldorf Astoria in New York. I like to come to Catfish Creek on vacation."

"You're homeless, aren't you," Lonnie said matter-of-factly.

Moses stopped laughing. "What gave you your first clue, Sherlock?"

"I've seen you standing by the bridge at the corner of I-27 and Peyton Avenue, panhandling."

His eyes crinkled with joy. "Ah, yeah, that's a real sweet spot. I usually make pretty good money there."

"How did you become homeless?" Lonnie asked. "I mean, if you don't mind telling me."

"You sure are a nosy parker," Moses said. "Now, I'll tell you what you wanna know, but information costs money." He rubbed his fingers together. "You positive you ain't got any on you?"

Knowing he would have to give him something in order to keep the conversation going, Lonnie pulled out his wallet and removed a dollar bill from it.

Moses made a face. "What am I supposed to do with that? Blow my nose with it? C'mon, kid. You can do better than that." He snatched the wallet away from Lonnie and took out the rest of the money. Tossing the wallet back, he said, "Okay, what do you wanna know?"

After his aggressive behavior, Lonnie wasn't sure he wanted to keep talking to him. But Moses had his thirteen dollars. "How did you end up on the streets?"

Moses grinned, as if he was about to answer with something sarcastic, but then his grin faded. He looked down and shook his head. "Bad decisions, kid. Bad decisions."

"What kinds of bad decisions?"

"Bad decisions don't come in different kinds," he said. "Bad is bad."

"I guess what I want to know is, what was your life like before you became homeless? Did you have a job? A family? A house?"

"Yeah, I had all those things, but I lost them all."

"How?"

"Why are you asking me all this?" Moses asked, now sounding irritated. "You writing a book or something?"

"No, sir, but . . . um . . . well, I have to write a research paper for school, and I thought I'd pick homelessness as my topic."

That fib seemed to calm him down. Or maybe it was that Lonnie had called him *sir* again.

"Okay, professor, here's your scoop. For me, it was the drink. I started drinking when I was in high school, and I never stopped."

"Do you, um . . . do you do drugs?"

Moses glowered at him. "Do I look like a druggie to you, kid?"

"No, sir. I was just asking . . . "

"I ain't stupid. Like I said, I made a lot of bad decisions, but that wasn't one of them."

"What about your family? Were you married? Do you have children?"

"Yeah, I got a wife and a daughter somewhere, but I ain't seen them in years."

"What about your job? What kind of work did you do?"

Moses paused for a moment, as if he was probing his mind for a forgotten memory. "I worked at a furniture store warehouse," he said. "Made a good living out of it, too."

"Did you lose your job 'cause of your drinking?"

"Naw. The place shut down and everybody got laid off. But it was the drink that kept me from finding more work." Moses looked up at the sky. The clouds had begun to grow dark and thick. "We'd better go inside before it starts to rain."

"Inside? Where?" Lonnie asked, looking around Catfish Creek.

"C'mon, I'll show you."

Moses led him down to the edge of the water. Then they crossed over to the other side by stepping on large stones. They walked up a grassy hill and went through an opening in the underbrush, which looked like a long tunnel.

When they reached the end, Lonnie saw a white stone building with a wooden arched doorway, like those in storybook houses. It struck him odd that in all the times he had been to Catfish Creek, he had never noticed the building.

"Where are we?" he asked.

"Welcome to the Hold, kid," Moses said. "You wanted to know where I live. Well, this is it." He opened the door, and a strong odor, like the smell of wet newspapers mixed with the stench of urine and feces wafted out. "Yeah, I know. It takes some getting used to," he added, when he saw the look on Lonnie's face.

Inside the Hold, dozens of haggard-looking homeless men, women and children wandered about, moaning and wailing, like unrepentant sinners condemned to hell. The building, empty of furniture, was littered with old mattresses, cardboard boxes and shopping carts. A gray patch of light, filled with dancing dust particles, seeped from a small window high above a wall. The only other source of light came from a metal barrel at the end of the room, crowned with flames. Several men stood around it, tossing pieces of wood inside the barrel to keep the fire going.

From the darkness, an old man with no legs rolled toward them on a wheelchair. He wore a camouflage cap and a camouflage jacket. Two plastic American flags were duct-taped to the back of his wheelchair.

"We got us a visitor, J.D.," Moses told him. "I don't know what his name is, though."

"That's okay," the old man said to Lonnie. "He don't know my name, either."

"But he just called you J.D."

"J.D.'s short for John Doe," the old man answered with a cackle, followed by a hacking cough.

"So what's your real name?"

"It don't matter. I've gone by so many names that one's just as good as the other."

"I've seen you before," Lonnie told him. "On Sterling Boulevard. You wheel yourself up and down the sidewalk, holding a sign that says HOMELESS VIETNAM VET."

Moses laughed. "J.D. ain't no Vietnam vet. He ain't never even been in the military."

J.D. certainly looked like a military veteran—a veteran who had fallen on hard times.

"Diabetes ate up my legs," J.D. confessed. "But folks are more likely to give me money if they think I lost them in the war than if I tell them the truth."

"So in other words, you're just conning people into giving you money," Lonnie said bluntly.

"What are you? A Polly Pureheart?" J.D. coughed again, then spat a greenish loogie on the floor. "You think I panhandle 'cause I'm trying to get rich off other folks? 'Cause I like it? Let me tell you something, sonny boy. You don't go through life doing only the things you wanna do. You do whatever you gotta do to survive, whether you like it or not, you understand? It's just something that's gotta be did."

A booming clap of thunder rattled the walls, followed by a *pat-pat-pat-pat* striking the roof.

J.D. cocked his head. "Sounds like it's starting to shoot rain. C'mon, let's go to the other side where the roof don't leak."

Moses took the handles of J.D.'s wheelchair and pushed him across the room while Lonnie walked behind them.

All of a sudden, a hand reached out from the shadows and grabbed his arm. A Mexican woman, wrapped in a black shawl, cried out desperately, "*Ayúdanos, por favor. Mis hijos tienen mucha hambre.* Please help us. My children are very hungry."

Tugging himself away, Lonnie said, "*Lo siento, pero no tengo dinero.* I'm sorry, but I don't have any money."

More hands reached out and yanked at his clothes — tiny hands with razor-sharp claws. "*¡Hambre! ¡Hambre! ¡Hambre!* Hungry! Hungry! Hungry!"

Lonnie looked down and saw a pack of little kids, no older than four or five. Their jaws snapped open as they tried to sink their pointy fangs into him. *"¡Hambre! ¡Hambre! ¡Hambre!"*

"J.D.! Moses! Help!" Lonnie screamed, but they had disappeared into the darkness.

"¡Hambre! ¡Hambre! ¡Hambre!"

The little monsters dragged him down to the floor and crawled on top of him, biting and clawing at his face, his arms and his body.

Lonnie opened his eyes. He sat up in his bed. No, it wasn't his bed. Where was he?

His dad's snoring brought him back to reality. They were in a room at a place called the Twin Oaks Motel, and Lonnie was lying on the double bed next to his dad's.

He got up to use the restroom, and then returned to bed, no longer sleepy.

The week after Thanksgiving, he and his dad moved their possessions from their house to a public storage shed that was too small to hold everything, but it was all they could afford. Whatever didn't fit—a couch, Lonnie's bedroom furniture, the china cabinet and the dining room set—was divided between Joe and Mario, who squeezed them inside their garages. Lonnie and his dad spent their last night at the house sleeping on the floor.

The following day, Lonnie's dad picked him up from school and drove him to their new residence, a white stone building with brown trim. The paint was peeling off in places, and the roof looked as if it was about to cave in. The motel parking lot was cratered with pot holes, and Lonnie's dad had to drive carefully to avoid them.

He had chosen the Twin Oaks Motel because it was the least ratty place he could find for the price. Lonnie hated to have seen what the other motels his dad scouted out looked like.

Although the outside appeared as if it was ready for demolition, their room was surprisingly decent. It had two double beds, a dresser with a TV sitting on top, a nightstand, a table with two chairs, a small fridge and a microwave. But it wasn't home. It would never be home.

"We're just gonna stay here for a few days, that's all," Lonnie's dad said. "I promise."

"Yeah, yeah, I know. Until you find a job," Lonnie said critically.

"Look, buddy, I know you're mad at me, and I guess you got a right to be. But I ain't doing this on purpose. This is the best I can do right now, so don't knock it, okay? Things are gonna get better. You just have to be patient."

"I'll try not to hold my breath waiting," Lonnie muttered and walked out the door.

He was sick of him. Lonnie didn't know what his dad's problem was. He had been out of work for almost a year. Surely he could have found something by now. Anything! Lonnie had begun to wonder if his dad was really trying to find a job. Or could it be that he didn't want to work. Maybe he was just plain lazy.

Lonnie's mother used to think so. She would constantly nag her husband because he wouldn't help clean the house.

"*I'm not your slave, Richard. A marriage is a partnership, and you need to do your share of the work around here.*"

"*I do my share. More than my share. You think trucking's easy? Try it for a week, and see if you still think I don't do my share of the work.*"

"*I'm talking about housework, Richard.*"

"*That's your responsibility. I don't do women's work.*"

The motel didn't have a lobby, only a small office with an EMPLOYEES ONLY sign on the door. Next to the office door was a counter with a bullet-proof glass window and a small arched opening where transactions were conducted.

Around the corner of the building, a green sign with white lettering was screwed onto the wall, listing the Twin Oaks Motel rules:

NO TRESPASSING
NO LOITERING
NO WEAPONS
NO PROSTITUTION
NO DRUG DEALING
NO PUBLIC ALCOHOL CONSUMPTION

If Cousin Rita was to see the sign, Lonnie could imagine her saying, "Oh, my *gatos!*"

If his mother knew where they were now living, he could picture her turning to his dad and saying, "My God, Richard. What have you done?"

CHAPTER NINETEEN

WHEN THEY LIVED IN THEIR HOUSE, Lonnie could hole up in his room for hours, doing his homework, watching TV, listening to music or talking on the phone. But in their cramped motel room, where they had been staying for the past two weeks, there was no place he could be alone, except for a tiny bathroom he had to share with his dad.

Concentrating on his studies was almost impossible because his dad had the TV on all the time. He would lie on top of his bed, drinking beer, while Lonnie sat at the table, trying to get his assignments done.

Since they didn't have a stove or a regular oven, their meals consisted mainly of sandwiches and microwaveable foods. On occasion, Lonnie's dad would send him to the nearby Taco Bell or McDonald's to pick up something for them to eat.

At one time, Lonnie couldn't wait for school to end. As soon as classes let out, he would hurry out of the building and race home. Now, Wyatt Middle School had become his only place of refuge, and he dreaded having to be picked up from there, only to be driven back to the hell-hole known as the Twin Oaks Motel.

Axel told Lonnie he had seen a FOR RENT sign in front of his house and wanted to know why he hadn't mentioned that they had moved.

"We decided to move, that's all."

"Oh, yeah. Lots of sad memories there, right?" Axel said sympathetically.

"I guess you could say that."

"So where are you living now?"

"It's kind of far," Lonnie said. "Listen, I'd rather not talk about it 'cause our place is out of district, and I don't want the office to find out where we live, or they might make me transfer to another school in the middle of the year."

"Gotcha, man. I won't say anything."

Christmas break was coming up, which worried Lonnie because it meant that he would be spending every minute of each day in the motel room with his dad, like prison inmates, with nothing to do.

Hate is too strong a word for how Lonnie felt toward his dad. He didn't hate him, but he did hate what he was doing to them with the choices he was making.

A perfect solution dangled within his grasp. His dad could still swallow his pride and admit to his family that they needed help. Then they could move to Abilene and live with his parents in their four-bedroom house. They could each have their own room, and Lonnie could go to school with his cousins, while his dad looked for a job, either in Abilene or in nearby towns, like Eastland or Ranger. But each time Lonnie brought up the idea, his dad shot it down.

With each passing day, Lonnie's resentment toward him continued to grow. His dad had become a fat, pathetic man, always stinking of beer and body odor. He hadn't shaved for weeks, and his hair had grown down to his shoulders. No wonder he couldn't find a job. If Lonnie was the boss of a company, he wouldn't hire him, either.

He recalled a phone conversation he once heard between his mother and his grandma Salinas in which his mother was complaining about her husband.

"We're drifting apart, Mami. Richard acts like he's still in high school, and sometimes I feel as if I'm raising two kids instead of one."

Lonnie now understood what she had been going through. He used to think his dad was real cool. His dad would say a lot of stupid, silly things that would make Lonnie's mother groan, but they always cracked Lonnie up. Whenever his dad ran errands, he would invite Lonnie to go with him, and he loved to tag along.

They shared common interests: horror movies, TV shows, comic books and sports. His dad had taught him how to play the guitar, and even though Lonnie wasn't good at it, his dad made him feel as if he was the best musician in the world.

Looking back, Lonnie realized that the reason his dad had been so much fun to be with was because he had turned over all parental responsibilities to his wife. He had been more interested in being Lonnie's buddy than a dad. But if God had intended for him to be his buddy, he would have made him his age.

What Lonnie needed was a parent who would look after him, who would make sure he was well-taken care of. Yet somewhere along the way, their roles had been reversed. Lonnie had become the dad, and his dad had become the irresponsible, unmotivated, thirteen-year-old.

They weren't living; they simply existed. They were like zombies, wandering around aimlessly. Without purpose. Without promise. Without hope.

More than once, Lonnie considered calling his grandparents Rodríguez to make them aware of their situation.

Yet, despite their living conditions, he couldn't betray his dad. He couldn't go behind his back. His dad had gotten them into this mess, and one way or another, he was going to have to get them out of it.

Hoping to find something that would bring him comfort, Lonnie leafed through a Gideon's Bible he found in the nightstand drawer in their motel room. He thought about church. As much as he hated going there, he had begun to miss it. It may have been merely his desire to escape from his one-room prison cell, but Lonnie felt an urge to return to Mrs. Finley's Sunday school class. And after Sunday school, he would sit in the sanctuary during the preaching and not sneak off to Catfish Creek.

Lonnie's grandparents Salinas called. They invited him to dinner and to view Christmas lights. His dad agreed to let him go, but with one stipulation: "Tell them to pick you up at your school, and then have them drive you to Gilly's house when you're done. Tell them that I'll be there all night, jamming with Los Brujos, and that I'll take you home."

He didn't come right out and tell Lonnie to lie to his grandparents. He didn't have to. Lonnie knew he had to keep their new living quarters a secret from them. One slip up and they would sic CPS on his dad and try to take custody of Lonnie. But no matter how bad things got, living with his grandparents Salinas was not an option he wanted to consider.

His grandparents treated him to a Mexican restaurant called La Paloma Blanca, a place his grandpa claimed served the best enchiladas in town. He was right about that. Or maybe it was that Lonnie hadn't had a decent meal since Thanksgiving, because he practically licked his plate clean.

He noticed that some of the busboys who worked at the restaurant didn't appear to be any older than he was. Perhaps he could get a job doing something like that. La Paloma Blanca was too far from the Twin Oaks Motel, but there were other restaurants much closer. Maybe he could find work in one of the nearby fast-food joints. His dad had complained that those places were only interested in hiring kids. Lonnie thought he stood a better chance of finding a job than his dad did. Not only would he be earning money, he would also have something to do during the Christmas break.

After dinner, his grandpa drove them through the R Streets, one of the most affluent neighborhoods in Marsville. Lonnie's dad insisted that the R stood for "rich," but the neighborhood was known as the R Streets because many of the streets began with the letter R: Ramsey Street, Rutger Street, Ravinia Drive, Renaud Circle, Rosen Avenue.

The houses and trees were decorated with bright, colorful lights. All sorts of Santa Clauses were displayed, some standing and waving, others sitting on sleighs being pulled by reindeer. There were lighted candy canes, Christmas trees and holly wreaths. One house had a large sign that said WELCOME TO THE NORTH POLE. Below it, a team of mechanical elves built toys in Santa's workshop. On other lawns, choirs of angels and nativity scenes were set up.

Looking at Christmas lights saddened Lonnie because it reminded him that they no longer had a house to decorate. Each year, he and his parents would trim the outside of their house with lights. They would also buy the fattest Christmas tree they could find and stand it up in front of their bay window. As Christmas Day neared, the bottom of the tree would begin to fill with presents, and Lonnie could hardly wait to see what he was going to get.

This year, they wouldn't hang any Christmas lights. They wouldn't buy a Christmas tree. And for the first time, Lonnie didn't expect to receive any Christmas presents.

After his grandpa dropped him off at Gilly's, Lonnie shared his idea of looking for a job with his dad.

"It won't hurt to try," he said half-heartedly, thinking that his son wouldn't have a better chance of finding a job than he did.

The following afternoon, Lonnie's dad picked him up from school and drove him to the motel, but he didn't go inside.

"I'm gonna go out for a while," he said. "Here's ten bucks. When you get hungry, get yourself something to eat."

"Where are you going?" Lonnie asked.

"If you need anything, call me," he said, ignoring Lonnie's question. "Good luck with your job hunting."

Lonnie's only homework assignment was to write an essay titled "How Do You Plan to Spend the Winter Holidays?" He had no idea what he and his dad would be doing during the break, or even where they would be living. So he made up a story about how they were going to celebrate Christmas and New Year's Day with his cousins in Abilene. For him, that would be the perfect way to spend the holidays.

As soon as Lonnie finished his homework, he headed down the street to Brownie's Coffee Shop, hoping they might be able to use a busboy or a dishwasher. He had never applied for a job, so he wasn't sure what to expect.

The cashier greeted him with a pleasant smile and invited him to sit wherever he wanted. When Lonnie told her he was looking for a job, her smile disappeared and she told him to sit on a bench by the entrance.

Lonnie waited. And waited. And waited. Customers came in and out, and the cashier flashed them that same phony smile she had given him.

Forty minutes later, a man in a suit entered the coffee shop. He went around the counter and spoke briefly with the cashier, who after a couple of minutes, pointed to Lonnie.

The man came over. "How old are you, son?"

"Thirteen."

The man shook his head. "Sorry, too young. Can't hire you."

"But I really need a job," Lonnie said.

"When do you turn fourteen?"

"Not until August."

"Come back and see me then," the man said. "The youngest the state will allow me to hire anyone is four-teen."

"Okay, thanks," Lonnie said, dejected.

As he started out the door, the man told him, "You might try getting a paper route. That's how I earned my money when I was your age."

A paper route might be something to consider. In the meantime, Lonnie crossed the street and walked to the Taco Bell, thinking he might have better luck at a fast-food place, but he got the same response. The manager said he would have to be fourteen before she could con-sider hiring him.

As long as he was there, he ordered four crispy tacos and a small Coke to go.

When he arrived at the Twin Oaks, he saw a man and a woman arguing in the parking lot, yelling and cussing at each other. Not wanting any part of it, Lonnie hurried inside his room and shut the door.

He sat his food on the table and was about to turn on the TV, when he heard the woman shriek, *"Aaaah! Somebody help me!"*

Lonnie opened the door and looked out. The man was dragging the woman by her hair across the parking lot. Her blouse was ripped open, and she was bleeding from her nose and mouth.

"Stop him! He's gonna kill me!" the woman screamed.

The man stared piercingly at Lonnie. "Go back inside, kid. You didn't see nothing, you understand?"

Lonnie's heart pounded madly and his breathing quickened. He slammed the door shut and turned off all the lights, hoping the man hadn't gotten a good look at him. He cracked open the curtain and saw the man throw the woman in the passenger side of a red Ford Mustang. Then he slid in the front seat and peeled out of the parking lot.

Lonnie started to call 911, but as he pulled his phone out of his pocket, he thought: *What if the man finds out I was the one who called the police?* The man knew where Lonnie was staying, the third room from the right. Lonnie had learned, from his mother's death, that witnesses could be permanently silenced.

He called his dad, but got no answer. He tried several more times. Nothing. Terrified, he curled up in his bed in a fetal position and lay there without eating his food.

Lonnie never reported what he saw that night to the police. Nor did he tell his dad. What could his dad have done about it? Call the cops? Lonnie had already nixed that idea.

And he never again saw the man, the woman or the red Ford Mustang.

What occurred outside his room that night remained Lonnie's secret—a dark and terrible secret that would haunt him for the rest of his life.

CHAPTER TWENTY

LONNIE DECIDED TO SKIP MATH TUTORING. As soon as the final bell rang, he flew out the doors without letting Mrs. Ridley know not to expect him. Hoping he wasn't too late, he ran down the sidewalk as fast as he could.

A few students were hanging around the front of Lamar Elementary School, waiting to be picked up. A teacher assistant, who was supervising them, eyed Lonnie briefly. She didn't appear to recognize him, which was understandable. She hadn't seen him in two years, and even then, she didn't know him well. Lonnie couldn't think of her name, but he remembered that she used to monitor the cafeteria during his lunch period.

Lamar seemed tiny now. The hallways felt narrower, and the ceiling appeared lower than the last time Lonnie was there. A Christmas tree, surrounded by gift-wrapped boxes, stood near the main office. Green and red paper chains were strung across the hallway. Pictures of Santa Claus, the art work of the first graders, were stapled to the walls.

Ms. Perlman, the office manager, was sitting on a bench outside the office talking with a parent. Before she had a chance to question Lonnie's reason for being there, he said, "I came to see Mr. Treviño."

She nodded an approval, and he went upstairs.

The door was open, but out of courtesy, Lonnie knocked before entering. To his disappointment, Mr. Treviño wasn't in his room. His blazer was draped behind his chair, which gave Lonnie hope that he hadn't left yet. Perhaps he was in a meeting or visiting with other teachers.

Stapled to the back wall of the room was a cardboard fireplace with Santa Claus' legs dangling from inside it. A caption above read: GUESS WHO'S COMING TO TOWN? Around the fireplace hung letters to Santa that the students had written.

Lonnie had done a similar activity when he was in Mr. Treviño's class, except that instead of a fireplace, his teacher had covered the wall with butcher paper and had painted a full-sized Santa Claus on it, holding a long list. Above the painting, the caption read: HE'S MAKING A LIST AND CHECKING IT TWICE. By fourth grade, no one in Lonnie's class believed in Santa Claus. Mr. Treviño had assigned them to write letters to Santa as a fun activity.

On a table by the window sat candy houses the students had made, using milk cartons as a base. Lonnie had done the same art project when they read Roald Dahl's *Charlie and the Chocolate Factory,* and he assumed Mr. Treviño's students were reading the book.

Lonnie's heart ached with nostalgia, thinking about how different his life had been three years earlier. He was making good grades, his mom was alive, his dad was working and they lived in a nice home. Never in a million years could he have imagined that he would be in the situation he was in now. He walked over to his old desk, the second one in the third row, and sat in it, wishing he could somehow turn back time, wishing he was still a fourth grader with no worries.

"Lonnie?"

He jumped, and a small gasp slipped out of his throat.

"What brings you here?" Mr. Treviño asked.

Lonnie quickly stood up. "Hi, sir. I just wanted to come by to say hello."

"Hello," Mr. Treviño said in a lively voice. Then his face turned grim. "I am deeply sorry about what happened to your mom. I first heard about it on the radio while I was driving to work, but I didn't make the connection until I saw her picture on the news. How are you and your dad doing?"

Lonnie's eyes watered up, and his lower lip began to quiver. "I . . . I think we're homeless."

CHAPTER TWENTY-ONE

WITHOUT INTERRUPTING, Mr. Treviño sat on top of a student desk and listened patiently, while Lonnie shared everything that had happened. Finally Mr. Treviño asked, "Have you spoken to one of the counselors at your school about this?"

"No, sir."

"Why not?"

"Just because," Lonnie said with a shrug. He liked Ms. Hoffman, but he didn't think she could do anything for him.

And Mr. Bigelow creeped him out. Once in a while, Lonnie would run into him in the hallways, and Mr. Bigelow would greet him with an overly cheerful clown smile and a pat on the back. "How's it going, Lon? *How th it going, Lon?*"

"Maybe you'd feel more comfortable talking to Ms. Clegg," Mr. Treviño suggested. "You remember her, don't you?"

Ms. Clegg was Lamar's guidance counselor. Once or twice a month, she would show up in Lonnie's classroom to present lessons, using puppets with names like Tookie Turtle and Pamela 'Possum. With everything he was going through, Lonnie didn't want advice from a hand puppet.

"I don't want to talk to her, either," he said. "And please don't tell her about me."

"I won't say anything without your permission," Mr. Treviño said, crossing his heart with a finger. "I promise. But I think you should know that Ms. Clegg has lots of experience working with homeless families. After all, we have a number of homeless children here at our school."

"You do?"

He nodded. "As a matter of fact, one of my students lives in a shelter with her two younger siblings and their mother. You'd never be able to tell it, though. Margie acts like any other child in my class."

"How did she and her family become homeless?" Lonnie asked.

"Margie has a situation similar to yours. Except that in her case, her parents divorced and Dad took off. Mom lost her job and has been unemployed ever since."

"Is that how people become homeless?" Lonnie asked. "By losing their job and not being able to find another one?"

Mr. Treviño took a quick peek at his watch, which led Lonnie to say, "If you need to leave, I understand. I didn't mean to take up so much of your time."

"No, no, I'm not in hurry. I just need to make a stop at the cleaners on the way home, but they don't close until six." Mr. Treviño stood and rolled out his teacher's chair, which was more comfortable than the student desk.

"There are lots of reasons why people become homeless," he said. "But here's something interesting, Lonnie. The panhandlers you see on the streets make up just a tiny fraction of the homeless population. Many homeless people live in motels or with friends or family members, who take them in temporarily, and they're making every effort to get back on their feet. You're not likely to see them on street corners begging for money. But as for what causes people to become homeless, I'd say it's mainly due to bad decisions they make in life."

"Yeah, I heard that somewhere," Lonnie said.

"I know it's easy to point a finger at the homeless and say, 'That's what you get,'" Mr. Treviño continued. "But some people become homeless through no fault of their own. A woman leaves an abusive relationship and has nowhere to go, for example."

"You know what's weird?" Lonnie said. "My dad likes to make fun of homeless people. He calls them druggies and con artists who are too lazy to find a job. But now we're homeless, too."

"Well, your dad isn't totally wrong," Mr. Treviño said. "Some homeless people *are* druggies and con artists. About a third of the street beggars here in Marsville are drug addicts or alcoholics. Another third are mentally ill. These are the people the city tries to help, by offering medical and social services. Then there are panhandlers the city refers to as 'entrepreneurial homeless.' Do you know what an entrepreneur is?"

"Isn't that like somebody who owns a business?" Lonnie asked, thinking back to a story he had read about Milton Hershey, the man who founded the Hershey's Chocolate Company.

"That's right. Well, some so-called homeless people really aren't homeless. They live in an apartment or in a rent house, and they receive some type of government assistance, like a monthly disability check. Panhandling is their business. That's how they supplement their income. The city has a hard time dealing with this group because they don't want to be helped. As far as they're concerned,

they have a job — panhandling. Then there are the dere-
licts who prefer to live on the streets rather than in a
shelter. They see themselves as modern-day cowboys
who sleep under the stars and make just enough money
to sustain themselves."

"They're *vagos*," Lonnie said.

Mr. Treviño smiled. "That's exactly what they are,
Lonnie. *Vagos*."

"How do you know so much about homeless people?" Lonnie asked.

"Well, our church works closely with the Helping
Hand, a homeless shelter downtown. Sometimes I volunteer there on Saturdays, so I guess I've learned a thing or
two about homelessness."

Lonnie looked up at the clock. It was almost five, and
tutoring time would be ending soon. "Excuse me, sir. I
need to make a quick phone call."

"Sure, go ahead."

Lonnie stepped into the hallway and called his dad.
Not wanting him to know where he was, he told him he
was staying late for tutoring, and asked if he could be
picked up at five-thirty.

When Lonnie reentered the classroom, he showed Mr.
Treviño his cell phone. "My dad needs his phone in case
somebody calls about a job, and I've been able to keep
mine 'cause it's part of his phone service package, and it
doesn't cost extra for me to have it."

"Don't put it away yet, Lonnie," Mr. Treviño said. He
drew his phone out of his pocket and scrolled through it.
"I have a number I want you to give your dad. It belongs
to Mr. Marriott."

"Mary who?" Lonnie asked.

"Marriott. You know, as in the hotel chain. George Marriott is a deacon at my church and a real good friend of mine. He's also the director of the Helping Hand. I'd like for your dad to call him. The Helping Hand has lots of social service programs that may be able to help you."

Lonnie added the number to his contacts list and then hesitatingly said, "Please don't take this the wrong way, sir, but I don't think my dad will call your friend."

"Why not?"

"That's just the way he is. He doesn't like to ask people for help."

Mr. Treviño leaned forward in his chair and stared intently at Lonnie. "Let me ask you something. Do you think your dad is suffering from depression?"

"I don't know," Lonnie said, although he'd had his suspicions for a long time.

"Sometimes when people become unemployed, they fall into a depression that keeps them from trying to find work. Your dad's heavy drinking, his lack of motivation and his feelings of hopelessness are signs of depression. The Helping Hand can provide counseling and even prescribe medication, if that's what he needs."

"I'll try to talk to him about it, sir."

"Good. In the meantime, be patient with your dad. Don't take your frustrations out on him. If he can't be strong for you, then you're going to have to be strong for him. Do you understand?"

Lonnie nodded weakly. He looked out the window. It was starting to get dark. He thanked Mr. Treviño for taking the time to talk to him. As he walked out of the room, he noticed a wreath hanging on the door. "Merry Christmas, sir," he said.

"*Feliz Navidad*," Mr. Treviño replied.

Lonnie ran back to his school, where his dad picked him up a short time later. Once again, he dropped him off at the Twin Oaks Motel and drove away without telling him where he was going.

After his dad left, Lonnie walked down the street to the Chicken Shack.

The Chicken Shack was a run-down, yellow and red building that had once been a Dairy Queen. Lonnie figured they might not be as picky about who they hired as the Brownie's Coffee Shop or the Taco Bell, so he crossed his fingers and hoped for the best.

The moment he entered the building, the smell of greasy chicken assaulted his senses. A man and a woman were standing by the counter, waiting for their food. A pimply-face kid poked his head out the ordering window and in a monotone voice said, "Welcome to the Chicken Shack. May I take your order?"

"Is the manager working tonight?" Lonnie asked.

"Why?"

"I'm looking for a job."

The kid handed the couple their chicken order, and they left to find a place to sit. "We ain't got no openings."

"Can I talk to the manager, anyway?"

"He don't get here till seven, but like I said, we ain't got no openings."

"You need a job?" Lonnie heard someone say.

He turned around and saw a man standing behind him, wearing a black suit, a white shirt and a red tie decorated with tiny Christmas trees.

"Are you the manager?" Lonnie asked.

"No, I need someone to rake my leaves," the stranger said. "My yard man quit on me, and my back's too worn out for me to get out there and do it myself. There's twenty-five dollars in it for you if you're interested."

The kid behind the counter stared at them, and Lonnie wondered if he was disappointed that someone had offered him a job.

"Sure, but, um . . . can you make it thirty-five?" Lonnie asked, remembering what his dad had said about negotiating price.

The stranger frowned, and for a second, Lonnie thought he had talked himself out of a job. "Tell you what. Let's start off with twenty-five, and if you do a real good job, I'll throw in the extra ten."

"Awesome. I'll have to check with my dad first, but I'm sure he'll let me do it. When do you want me to come over?"

"How about Saturday morning between eight-thirty and nine? That sound good to you?"

"Yes, sir."

"What's your name?"

"Lonnie Rodríguez."

"Lonnie, I'm Sam Porras." The man took a pen out of his shirt pocket and pulled a paper napkin from the napkin holder on the counter. He jotted down his name, address and phone number. "Talk to your parents, and if they say it's okay, call me."

After Lonnie left the Chicken Shack, he realized he had forgotten to buy something to eat. It was probably a good thing he didn't. As bad as it stunk in there, he couldn't imagine that their chicken was any good. Besides, he was too excited to eat. Twenty-five bucks for a couple of hours' work? More if he did a good job? He felt as if he had just struck gold.

CHAPTER TWENTY-TWO

LONNIE AND HIS DAD ROSE EARLY to eat breakfast at McDonald's. His dad was glad Lonnie had gotten a job, but he wanted to meet Sam Porras in person, although they had already spoken on the phone.

On the way to McDonald's, they stopped at a 7-Eleven, where Lonnie's dad bought ten dollars' worth of scratch-off lottery tickets. Lonnie thought it was a waste of money, but he didn't say anything. His dad was searching for answers, and if his only hope came in the form of lottery tickets, Lonnie had no right to tell him he couldn't buy them.

He mentioned the possibility of getting a paper route to earn extra money.

"No way, buddy. I'm not gonna have you out there at five o'clock in the morning, roaming the streets by yourself. It's too dangerous."

"Maybe you could take me in your car, and we could throw papers together," Lonnie said. "When we still subscribed to *The Monitor*, the paper guy used to deliver our newspaper from his van."

His dad took a sip of coffee to wash down his sausage biscuit. "I don't know about that. I'm driving your mom's clunker, and if it breaks down, I ain't got the money to fix it. Also, the price of gas keeps going up, so throwing papers by car don't seem worth the effort to me."

He had a good point. But as much as they were struggling financially, Lonnie thought he would be willing to give the paper route idea a try.

His dad took a quarter out of his pocket and scratched off his lottery tickets. But as Lonnie had come to expect, none of them paid off.

"All I need is one lucky break," his dad said, crumpling the worthless cards. "Just one lucky break."

Sam Porras' house wasn't far from the motel. It was an impressive white stucco house, with high arched windows and a red-clay tile roof. Palm trees stood at each end of the front door, and potted chrysanthemums lined the terra cotta steps. It amazed Lonnie how different the homes in Mr. Porras' neighborhood were compared to the low-rent motels a short distance away.

Lonnie rang the doorbell, but no one answered. He rang a couple of more times, then knocked.

At last, a woman came out, holding a cigarette between her fingers. "You Lonnie?" she asked in a smoker's voice.

"Yes, ma'am. And this is my dad."

"Come on in. I'm Thelma, Sammy's bookkeeper. Sorry I didn't hear you right away, but that doorbell's been busted for a while. I keep telling Sammy he needs to get it fixed, but you know how he is, always putting stuff off."

She led them through the kitchen and out the back door. "You here to help?" she asked Lonnie's dad.

"No, I'm just dropping off my son. Where's Mr. Porras?"

"At the club, I would imagine."

"The club?"

Thelma took a drag from her cigarette, then blew out a stream of smoke. "Sammy owns the Club Monte Carlo on Bickers Street, off I-27, which he might as well call home 'cause he's hardly ever here."

"Does he book bands?" Lonnie's dad asked hopefully.

"Sometimes. Why?"

"Hold on a second. I'll be right back." He rushed to his car, returning a moment later with a CD case in his hand. "I play in a Chicano band called Los Brujos," he told Thelma, handing her the demo CD. "I thought maybe Mr. Porras might be interested in booking us for some gigs at his club."

Thelma studied the CD cover. On it was a photo of Lonnie's dad, Gilly, Joe and Mario, posing with their instruments in front of what appeared to be a Spanish mission, but was actually the side of a restaurant called The Presidio.

"Well, Sammy usually uses DJs, but like I said, he does hire bands on occasion. I wouldn't get my hopes up too high, though. DJs are a lot cheaper to book than bands. Know what I mean?"

"I understand," Lonnie's dad said. "But can you give Mr. Porras my CD anyway?"

Thelma shrugged indifferently. "Sure."

Satisfied that Lonnie was in safe hands, he thanked her and left.

Thelma walked Lonnie to the shed and unlocked it. "Everything you need is in here," she said. "Rakes, trash bags, brooms, leaf blower."

"Yes, ma'am."

"When you fill the bags, sit them along the curb. The brush collectors are supposed to come by Monday to pick them up."

"Yes, ma'am."

"Felipe used to do the yard, but he had a family emergency in Mexico, so he had to leave right away. Until he comes back . . . if he comes back . . . Sammy needs someone to take Felipe's place. Think you can handle the work?"

"Yes, ma'am."

"And quit calling me ma'am. You make me feel old." Thelma took another puff of her cigarette, then tapped the ashes on the ground. "Sammy expects every leaf to be picked up. You got that?"

"Yes, ma'am . . . I mean, yeah, sure."

"I'll be in the study. When you're done, let me know, so I can pay you."

"Mr. Porras told me that if I did a real good job, he'd give me thirty-five dollars," Lonnie said, wanting to make sure they were clear on their agreement.

"Yes, he told me how you hustled the extra ten out of him." Thelma winked. "Good for you, Lonnie. I'll have your thirty-five dollars waiting for you when you're done."

The job turned out to be harder than Lonnie had expected. He didn't know when the last time was that Felipe had worked on the yard, but there were tons of leaves on the ground.

Rake, scoop and bag. Rake, scoop and bag.

After a while, his back was killing him. At one point, Lonnie felt like going inside the house and telling Thelma he didn't want to do it anymore. But they desperately needed the money, so he kept working.

Rake, scoop and bag. Rake, scoop and bag.

Three hours later, he finished, having filled and tied twenty-four bags. He called his dad to pick him up, then went inside to collect his money.

"Ma'am? Thelma?"

She didn't answer. Lonnie peeked inside the study, but she wasn't there. A laptop sat in the middle of a long, mahogany desk, along with a Diet Coke can, a half-eaten granola bar and a glass ashtray with a lit cigarette leaning inside it.

While Lonnie waited for Thelma to return, he studied the photos on the walls. He assumed the kids in the pictures were Mr. Porras' children and wondered if there was a Mrs. Porras. Thelma didn't mention her last name, but Lonnie didn't think she was Mr. Porras' wife.

His heart sank when he looked down and saw his dad's CD in the trash can. Despite what Thelma had said, she had no intention of giving it to her boss.

"Done already?"

Thelma's voice startled him. "Yes, ma'am . . . uh, Thelma. Do you want to take a look at what I did?"

She took the cigarette from the ashtray and slipped it in the corner of her mouth. "That's okay. I trust you." She reached into her trousers pocket and fished out thirty-five dollars. "Don't spend it all on girls," she said with a wink.

Lonnie jotted his name and phone number on a Post-it note and told Thelma to let Mr. Porras know that he was available to rake leaves anytime the work needed to be done.

He left, feeling terrific. Things were going to get better. He just knew they would.

CHAPTER TWENTY-THREE

On Sunday morning, Lonnie and his dad sat in the Winfield Road Presbyterian Church parking lot and gazed across the street at their old house. Another family was now living in it.

"We're gonna be back in a house real soon, buddy," Lonnie's dad said. "You'll see. Hopefully after Mr. Porras listens to my CD, he'll give Los Brujos a steady gig at his club."

It would never happen, but Lonnie didn't mention anything about Thelma throwing away the CD. "Want to go inside with me?" he asked.

"Nah, you go ahead. I got some things to do. You can pray for the both of us."

Lonnie slid out of the car, disappointed but not surprised. "Pick me up around twelve. If the service is still going on, I'll slip out quietly."

His dad drove off, and Lonnie returned to his Sunday school class for the first time in months. The lesson was about how Mary and Joseph had traveled from Nazareth to Bethlehem because they had to be registered in their hometown for a census the government was conducting. But when they arrived, they had no place to stay.

"It was like they were homeless," Lonnie told Mrs. Finley, then instantly regretted speaking out, thinking he may have said something inappropriate.

"That's an interesting thought," she said. "Would you care to elaborate?"

Lonnie glanced around the room, but nobody looked at him as if he had said the wrong thing. "Well, sometimes when homeless people don't have anywhere to go, they end up living under bridges or in abandoned buildings. In Mary and Joseph's case, they couldn't find a room at the inn, so they stayed in an animal stable, like they were homeless. But they knew they weren't going to live there permanently. They knew things were going to get better, the same as with a lot of homeless people. Things may be real bad for them, but they have to believe that their problems are only temporary."

"What an astute observation," Mrs. Finley said. "Thank you for sharing."

Lonnie wasn't sure what *astute* meant, but he liked the sound of the word. He left, thinking that he had as much to contribute to the Sunday school discussions as some of the know-it-alls in there, provided he didn't make any horror movie references.

He walked down the hallway and stopped by the rear window. Looking out, he realized that Catfish Creek had lost all its appeal for him. He no longer had any desire to hang out down there. And it wasn't because he was afraid of running into Moses or some other homeless person. He needed some consistency in his life, and church seemed like a good place for it.

Lighted Christmas wreaths with red bows hung on the walls of the sanctuary, and poinsettia plants lined the sides of the church stage. The pianist played Christmas carols, while the congregation made its way inside. A few ladies stopped and asked Lonnie how he was doing. He said fine, not caring to share what was really going on in his life.

He had planned to sit with some of the guys from his Sunday school class, but Jo Marie quickly scooted in his pew and sat next to him.

"I'm glad you're here, Lonnie," she said cheerily.

"Thanks. I'm glad to be here, too."

Jo Marie wasn't so bad, he decided. A little too churchy for his taste, but what did he expect with her dad being a preacher? After that day when he broke down in front of her, he felt as if they had grown closer.

Brother Beasley led the congregation in singing "Joy to the World." Lonnie never been much of a singer, but he belted out the words to each verse enthusiastically.

Brother Elrod preached a sermon titled "I'll Be Home for Christmas." With Christmas a week and a half away, Lonnie had no idea where he would be spending it. And it certainly wasn't going to be at "home."

After retelling the story of the birth of Jesus, Brother Elrod explained to the congregation that while Mary and Joseph weren't in their house at the time of the birth, they were still "home" because "home is wherever God is."

"Life is hard, but God is good," Brother Elrod emphasized as he concluded his message.

Lonnie turned to Jo Marie and said, "What an astute observation."

She gave him a curious look, not sure if he was putting her on.

After church, Lonnie and his dad ate lunch at the Wendy's near the motel, and Lonnie paid for their food with his leaf-raking money.

"How was church?" his dad asked.

"Alright, I guess."

"What'd they preach about?"

"Oh, the usual stuff. You know, about God and Jesus."

"That's good."

After lunch, they returned to the motel to watch football on TV. Lonnie dozed off midway through a game between the Tampa Bay Buccaneers and the Carolina Panthers, but he woke up in time to watch the Dallas Cowboys play the Miami Dolphins. He told his dad that they were running low on clean clothes, and could he take him to the Laundromat as soon as the game was over.

His dad cursed when a Cowboys receiver dropped what looked like a sure touchdown pass. "I don't know why I bother watching those stupid Cowgirls," he complained. "They always choke before the season's over."

"Did you hear what I said?" Lonnie asked.

"Yeah, yeah." His dad cursed again when the kicker missed a forty-two yard field goal try on the next play.

During the commercial break, Lonnie gathered their dirty clothes and stuffed them into trash bags. Then he sat back down and watched as the Cowboys continued to trail the Dolphins.

Finally, with six and a half minutes left in the fourth quarter, and with the Cowboys losing 38 to 14, his dad turned off the TV and grabbed his car keys from the dresser. "Come on, let's go."

Lonnie took the trash bags outside. His dad opened the car trunk and was about to help him load them in, when he heard someone say, "Hey, amigo. You got a light?"

Two men were standing behind them.

"Sorry, I don't smoke," Lonnie's dad said.

One of the men pulled out a gun and pointed it at his face. "Then how about giving us your money?"

CHAPTER TWENTY-FOUR

"C'MON, MAN, DON'T DO THIS," Lonnie's dad pleaded. "We're going through a real rough time right now."

"Yeah? Well, so are we. Now give me your wallet." The gunman turned his weapon on Lonnie. "You, too, little man. Empty your pockets."

It was dark, and Lonnie couldn't see the men's faces clearly, but the gunman looked familiar. For a second, he thought it was Kevin Williams, the man who had shot his mother. But it couldn't be him. Kevin Williams was dead.

The gunman's accomplice was a tall, slender, African-American man with an uncombed afro. Both men were dressed shabbily, and Lonnie wondered if they were homeless.

"Listen, I ain't worked in almost a year," Lonnie's dad said. "This is all the money we got."

"We ain't got time to listen to your crying," the gunman's accomplice said. "Do what Carl says before he shoots you both, and then takes your wallets anyway."

The gunman glared at him. "Why'd you call me by my name? I told you never to use our names."

"Let's just get the money and split," his accomplice said without acknowledging his mistake.

"Everything out of your pockets," the gunman ordered. "Now!"

Reluctantly, Lonnie and his dad took out their wallets, pocket change, cell phones and keys.

"Take 'em, Dewayne," the gunman said.

"I thought you said we weren't gonna use our names."

"Just take 'em!"

"Can you at least let us keep our car?" Lonnie's dad asked.

Carl chortled. "You think we want that piece of junk?" He peeked inside the trunk to make sure there wasn't anything of value in it. "Keep it, amigo."

Dewayne tossed the keys on the ground. He shoved the coins and cell phones in his pocket, and then counted the money in the wallets. "Dawg, Carl! They got almost six hundred bucks between them."

Carl smiled. He kept his gun pointed at them as he and his partner walked backwards. "A pleasure doing business with you, amigos," he said with a soldier's salute. Then they disappeared into the night.

Lonnie and his dad stood speechless, too stunned to react to what had just happened. Lonnie's dad's entire unemployment check money was gone. So was Lonnie's leaf-raking money. They couldn't even go back inside their motel room to call the police because their key cards were in their wallets.

Lonnie's dad's face crumpled, and he began to sob. "I can't take this no more. We got nothing left. Nothing!" His knees buckled, and Lonnie had to hold him by the waist to keep him from falling. "I don't know what to do no more. I just . . . " The tone in his voice changed from sobbing to loud, animal-like howls. He pounded the hood of his car with his fists and screamed at the top of his lungs, "*God, help me!*"

As much as Lonnie wanted to cry too, he couldn't. He had to be strong for his dad, like Mr. Treviño had advised. "Let's go to the office and tell them what happened," he said. "They can call the police for us."

"What good do you think that's gonna do? You think the cops are gonna get our money back?"

Lonnie had already made a mistake by not calling the police when he should have, and he wasn't going to make the same mistake again, whether or not their money could be recovered. With his arm around his dad, he walked him to the office. Finally his dad composed himself and dried his tears.

No one was at the window, but there was a bell on the counter with an index card that read RING BELL FOR SERVICE. In the back room, Lonnie could hear the TV blaring. Whoever was working the desk was watching the game.

He hit the bell several times. The TV volume became mute, and a man appeared at the window. He looked irritated, and Lonnie heard him mutter something about the Dallas Cowboys.

"Can I help you?"

"We just got robbed at gunpoint!" Lonnie told him. "We need you to call the police."

"Was it two of them? A white guy and a black guy?" the clerk asked, sounding almost bored.

"Yeah. How did you know?"

The clerk sighed. "This is the third time those guys have robbed our tenants. What do they think this place is, anyway? The First National Bank?"

"We also need new key cards to get back in our room," Lonnie said. "They took our wallets with our key cards in them."

"Well, you know there's a five-dollar charge for lost key cards," the clerk said.

"We didn't lose them. They were stolen."

"We still gotta replace them, lost or stolen." The clerk turned to Lonnie's dad. "I'll add the cost of the cards to your weekly rent, which, FYI is due tomorrow."

He picked up the phone and called 911. "Yeah, this is Floyd Womack, the manager at the Twin Oaks Motel, 6211 Freestone Avenue. Seems like we had another robbery here." He paused and asked Lonnie, "Anyone get hurt?"

"No, sir."

"Naw, they're all right. They just got their wallets stolen, that's all."

"And our cell phones," Lonnie said.

"And their cell phones. Yeah, I'll be here all night. I suppose they will, too." He asked Lonnie, "Y'all aren't planning to go anywhere tonight, are you?"

"I don't think so." With their money gone, they wouldn't be able to do their laundry or even go out to buy dinner.

"Yeah, okay. Thanks." The clerk hung up. He looked for Lonnie's dad, who was hidden in the shadows. "They're sending out a squad car. In the meantime, I guess you need to get back in your room. Which one are you in?"

"One-thirteen," Lonnie said.

"You want one key or two?"

"One."

The clerk handed Lonnie the new key card, and he and his dad walked back to their room to wait for the police.

Lonnie dropped the dirty clothes bags on top of the table. His dad sat on the edge of his bed, hunched over, and ran his fingers through his hair. "I don't know what to do," he said. "We can't stay here after tonight. They want the rent a week in advance, and I ain't got the money for it."

"Do you think you could borrow the money from somebody?" Lonnie asked.

"How will I pay it back? I don't get a check for another two weeks, and we can barely make it on that money without having to pay back a loan." His dad lay on his bed with his hands clasped behind his head and stared at the ceiling. "You know what? I think maybe it's time for you to go live with your grandparents, buddy. They were right. You need to stay with them till I can get back on my feet, and that might take a while."

"No, I want to stay with you," Lonnie said. "Come on, we'll figure something out." What really frightened him was what would become of his dad if he was left alone. Lonnie worried he might lose hope completely and end up like Moses. "We still have all our furniture and things in storage. Maybe you can sell some of it."

"If I do, I'll have to find a buyer real quick, 'cause I gotta let the front desk know by noon that we're staying, and they'll expect me to pay for the room at that time."

"If by some chance you can't come up with the money, do you think we could stay with one of your friends?" Lonnie asked.

"That ain't gonna work, buddy. If we could've stayed with them, I wouldn't have brought you to this flea bag motel. But they got their families. They ain't got no room for us."

Choosing his words carefully, Lonnie said, "I only have a few days of school left before the semester ends, and it wouldn't be a problem for me to transfer to another school in January."

His dad sat up. "What are you getting at?"

"Well, at one time you were thinking about us moving to Abilene. We could drive there tomorrow and stay with your parents. I'd miss a few days of school, but we're not doing a whole lot right now, with Friday being the last day before the Christmas break."

"No! I'm not gonna go back there and grovel at their feet, begging for scraps."

"Dad, I don't get it. You were thinking about doing that at Thanksgiving."

"Yeah, but you saw how they treated me. I'll always be the *burro* of the family. I don't wanna go back to Abilene till I can show them that I don't need their help."

There was a knock at the door, followed by a voice that said, "Marsville Police."

Lonnie's dad invited the two officers in and gave them a detailed account of what happened.

"We heard their names," Lonnie said, thinking he had an important clue that would help the police catch the robbers. "One guy's name is Carl and the other one's name is Dewayne."

"Carl Muncie and Dewayne Smalls," one of officers said, deflating Lonnie's excitement.

"You know who they are?" Lonnie's dad asked.

"Yeah, they're a couple of drifters who've been hitting the area. So far, they haven't hurt anyone. They just take what they want and go. We've been trying to catch them, but they work pretty fast."

The second officer added, "All we can tell you is that we'll step up patrol here in the east side. Hopefully we can stop them before they decide to do something really stupid."

After the police left, Lonnie's dad opened the fridge, took out a can of beer and sat in a chair. "First thing tomorrow, I'll get our phones deactivated," he said. "The only thing is, the phone store's not gonna replace our phones for free, and I ain't got the money to pay for new ones." He shook his head in disgust. "I ain't got money to pay for nothing."

"But you're going to sell some of our things tomorrow," Lonnie said. "We made pretty good money from our yard sale, and our furniture's worth a lot more than the stuff we sold then."

His dad replied bitterly, "Or maybe I'll just stand on a street corner with a cardboard sign that says HOMELESS. PLEASE HELP. GOD BLESS."

CHAPTER TWENTY-FIVE

LONNIE TRIED TO REMAIN FOCUSED on his studies, despite not knowing where he would be spending the night. He bowed his head, while pretending to read a book, and asked God to help his dad raise the money and also to help him find a job.

At one time, he might have confided in Axel about what they were going through, but now they seemed like total strangers.

Yvette asked him how he was doing, and he told her he was doing fine. She said good and walked away. Lonnie knew she was only being polite. She wasn't really interested in him, especially not after he saw her making out with Michael de Luna on the stairwell.

During passing period, Jo Marie reminded Lonnie of the Youth Christmas Party being held at the church Sunday night. A party would certainly be a lot more fun than sitting in their motel room watching TV. He told her he would try to make it.

When his dad picked him up from school, the first thing Lonnie asked was, "Were you able to sell our furniture?"

He drove away, staring straight ahead with both hands on the wheel.

"Were you?"

"Yeah, I sold some of it."

"And?"

He slapped the steering wheel. "I got eighty-seven bucks! That's it. People treated me like I was some kinda crook trying to sell stolen merchandise."

Looking at his disheveled appearance, Lonnie could believe it.

"I had to put gas in the car, so there went a good chunk of the money. And then I had to buy a disposable cell phone that I'll have to use till I can afford a better one."

"Do you have enough money left for us to stay at the motel tonight?" Lonnie asked.

"Yeah, but what are we gonna do tomorrow? And the next day? And the day after that?" he asked, his face haggard with worry. "I got our clothes and things in the trunk. I had to move us out of our room 'cause I couldn't pay for it by noon, and I didn't sell nothing till after one o'clock. I guess I could still go back and check us in again, but that place just ain't safe."

"So what are we going to do?"

"I don't know. Maybe Gilly will let us sleep in his house on the floor or something."

≋ ≋ ≋

Lonnie had an idea, but he couldn't remember the man's name. Mercer? Murphy? He had entered the name and number in his phone, but now it was gone. Marlow? Martin? Marriott. That's it! Marriott, as in the hotel chain.

"Dad, I think I know somebody who can help us." Lonnie told him about his visit with Mr. Treviño and his suggestion that they contact Mr. Marriott at the Helping Hand.

"Why are you talking to a teacher about our problems? You ain't got no business spilling family secrets."

"Dad, we need help."

"Well, I ain't gonna go to no shelter, I can tell you that right now."

"So you'd rather sleep on Gilly's cold floor? You told me he doesn't even want us staying with them. Or maybe you think we ought to sleep under the I-27 bridge with Moses."

His dad didn't answer.

"I really think we should check out the Helping Hand. Mr. Treviño seems to feel that it's an okay place, and I trust him. Please?"

His dad continued to drive in silence. Finally, when he stopped at a light, he asked, "Where is it?"

"Mr. Treviño said it's downtown on Main Street."

His dad turned the car around and they headed to the shelter.

As soon as he pulled into the parking lot, mobs of homeless men flocked around his car.

"Hey, partner, can you take me to my sister's house?"

"Amigo! Amigo! How about giving me a lift to Michigan Avenue?"

"The bus is running late, and I gotta get to the unemployment office before it closes."

Lonnie's dad shooed them away, and the men scattered like pigeons, but not before cussing him out for not giving them a ride.

"I don't know about this, buddy," he said warily, staring at the brown building.

Lonnie wasn't sure if he had made the right decision, either. When Mr. Treviño told him about the Helping Hand, he envisioned a nice, clean place where staff members with cheerful smiles would be ready to welcome them with open arms.

Instead, they saw lots of dirty, smelly, homeless people, mostly men, milling about the front doors of the shelter. Some sat on the railings with their legs dangling. Others walked up and down the steps, waiting for the doors to open. Many of them passed the time by talking to one another, but others stared blankly with glazed eyes.

And there was smoking. Smoking. Smoking. Almost everyone had a cigarette in their hand. As destitute as these people were, they somehow found the means to support their habit.

It frightened Lonnie to be there, but he didn't say anything. He was the one who was insistent on going to the shelter. Even if they found another place to spend the night, they would eventually have to come back here. So he gritted his teeth and kept his head down, refusing to meet anyone's eyes.

At four o'clock, the doors opened, and everyone made their way inside.

The first thing Lonnie noticed when he walked in was how clean the shelter was. The floors and walls were spotless and gave off a strong smell of lemon-scented disinfectant. Lonnie and his dad walked through a metal detector. After that, they were told to sign their names in a book sitting on a table.

"Are you first-timers?" the man at the table asked Lonnie's dad.

"Yeah, we're here to see . . . what's the man's name, buddy?"

"Mr. Marriott."

"Okay, but since you're first-timers, I need you to go to intake," the man said.

"What's that?" Lonnie's dad asked.

"That's where they take down your information. It's right over there."

"Can't we just talk to Mr. Marriott?"

The man snapped his fingers and pointed to the intake center. "Come on, pal. You're holding up the line."

They walked to the counter where a woman asked if she could help them.

"We're here to see Mr. Marriott," Lonnie's dad told her.

"Does he know you're coming?" she asked.

"He's expecting us," Lonnie said.

She picked up the phone receiver and asked Lonnie's dad, "What's your name?"

"Um . . . can you tell Mr. Marriott that Lonnie Rodríguez and his dad are here?" Lonnie asked. "Tell him I was Mr. Treviño's student."

The woman punched a button on the cradle and waited. "Mr. Marriott? I've got a boy and a man here who say they've got an appointment to see you."

"We don't have an appointment," Lonnie said. "Please tell him that Mr. Treviño sent us here."

"The boy says that a Mr. Treviño told him to come here. Yes, sir. I'll do it right away." The woman hung up. "Okay, go down that hallway. It's the last door on the left."

They started toward Mr. Marriott's office, but he stepped out to greet them. Mr. Marriott was a heavy-set man with thinning white hair and a friendly face.

"A pleasure to meet you both," he said, "although I wish it was under better circumstances."

He invited them into his office, and Lonnie and his dad sat in the two chairs facing his desk.

"Adam Treviño speaks very highly of you, Lonnie," Mr. Marriott said. "He also shared some things about what you've been going through. This is why we have the Helping Hand, to assist people such as yourselves who are struggling."

"We don't plan to stay here long," Lonnie's dad told him. "We got robbed of all our money, but I'm gonna get an unemployment check in a couple of weeks. Then I can find us another place."

"That's exactly the right attitude to have," Mr. Marriott said. "While we're here to help the indigent and the needy, the Helping Hand isn't meant to be a comfortable place. We provide shelter, but this isn't a flop house."

Although his face was cheerful, and his voice was calm, Mr. Marriott spoke with authority. He didn't look like a man who could be intimidated easily. Lonnie was sure he could be tough, especially when dealing with some of those scary people he had seen.

"We're not going to try to rush you out of here, Mr. Rodríguez. You decide how long you want to stay, but let me explain our policies." Mr. Marriott glanced at Lonnie. "We have family rooms for women and their children, but we don't have a children's section per se. Ordinarily we'd call Child Protective Services to put Lonnie in foster care, where he would stay until you can find something more suitable. But your son's at the age where we could go either way. I'll let him stay with you in the men's dormitory, provided you keep an eye on him at all times."

"You don't have to worry about that," Lonnie's dad told him.

"There's also a ten-dollar charge per night," Mr. Marriott said. "You can pay for your stay, or you can work it off. That's what some of our clients do. Almost every worker here is homeless, from the attendant at the table where you signed in, to the clerk at the intake center. The cooks and the servers in the cafeteria, most of them are homeless, too."

"I don't mind working," Lonnie's dad said. "Like I told Lonnie, it ain't that I don't wanna work. I just can't find nobody who'll hire me."

"Well, if you prefer to work for your stay, we can certainly find something for you to do," Mr. Marriott said. "As you know, our doors open at four, but everyone is expected to be out of the shelter by six the next morning. We want our clients up no later than five so they can shower, get dressed, eat breakfast and then be on their way."

"Where do they go once they leave here?" Lonnie's dad asked.

"Again, the Helping Hand is not a flop house," Mr. Marriott reiterated without answering the question. "We don't want our clients spending all day here, doing nothing. We do make exceptions, though. The sick and the elderly can stay. So can anyone who's attending our in-house drug-treatment programs. But for the most part, we expect our clients to go out and look for jobs."

Lonnie found out later that most homeless people at the Helping Hand didn't spend the day job-hunting. At six o'clock, they spread over the downtown area to panhandle. Or they might go down the river bottoms to homeless encampments. Others staked out their spots under bridges or street corners with their cardboard signs.

"Some companies offer catch-out jobs, and that's one way our clients earn money," Mr. Marriott said.

"What's a catch-out job?" Lonnie's dad asked.

"Catch-out is a term our clients use. It means day labor." Mr. Marriott turned to the window, and Lonnie and his dad looked out with him. "Trucks and vans will pull up to that vacant lot across the street. Our clients call it the catch-out gap. The drivers will announce something like, 'We need ten workers.'"

"What kinds of jobs do they have for them?" Lonnie's dad asked.

"Nothing pleasant, I can assure you. Factory work, construction, roofing, that sort of thing. But these are not forty-hour-a-week jobs, if that's what you're thinking. The reason our clients take them, regardless of what they may be, is because they get paid the same day they work."

"So if I decide to take one of those catch-out jobs, what do I do with my boy?" Lonnie's dad asked. "I don't want him here by himself."

"We have the Flournoy Center, which is just down the street. Basically, it's a child care facility where our clients' children can stay when they're not in school, or when they can't be accompanied by a parent. The center has a bus that will take Lonnie to school and pick him up if you can't do it."

"Looks like you got all your bases covered," Lonnie's dad said. "Listen, I got our stuff in the trunk of my car. Where do you want me to put it?"

"I'll give you a tour of the place in just a moment," Mr. Marriott said. "But let me explain to you that the Helping Hand is more than an overnight shelter. We offer a number of services, such as mental health care programs and Alcoholics Anonymous, which I strongly recommend you attend to help you with your drinking problem."

Lonnie's dad glared at his son. "Who says I have a drinking problem?"

"Do you have a drinking problem, Mr. Rodríguez?"

He shrugged. "I like to drink, sure, same as the next guy, but . . . look, all we need right now is a place to stay, that's all. I don't wanna go to no programs."

Mr. Marriott sighed. "Let me show you around then."

CHAPTER TWENTY-SIX

HE TOOK THEM TO THE CAFETERIA. It resembled the one at Lonnie's school. Long lines of men, women and a few children snaked along the walls of each side of the room, waiting to be fed.

Mr. Marriott introduced Lonnie's dad to Jerry Parnell, the cafeteria manager. Jerry, as he told them to call him, said that sure, he could always use the extra help.

Afterward, they took the elevator to the third floor, where Mr. Marriott showed them one of the men's dorms. The room had rows of bunk beds, most of them already occupied by grungy, beaten-down men, who sized them up and down as soon as they entered. Next to the dorm was the shower room, a large, open area with multiple showerheads, like the one in Lonnie's school gym. The shower room offered no privacy, and a number of men were bathing in there without any sense of modesty.

Lonnie had long gotten over his shyness of showering in front of the guys at school, but there was no way he was going to bathe in the same room as those men.

They got back in the elevator and rode down to the basement, where Mr. Marriott showed them the laundry room, which was lined with rows of coin-operated washers and dryers. There was a sign-up sheet, so Lonnie wrote down his name to reserve a wash time.

After Mr. Marriott left, Lonnie and his dad took the trash bags out of their car. They carried them up to the third floor and stuffed them inside their assigned locker. Then they made their way to the cafeteria, where beef burritos, pinto beans, salad, sliced peaches and iced tea were being served.

As soon as Lonnie's dad finished eating, he spoke with Jerry Parnell. Lonnie sat, mildly amused, watching his dad do "women's work," clearing dirty dishes off the tables and carrying them away in gray plastic tubs to the dishwashing area.

While his dad worked, Lonnie decided to get started on their wash. He asked his dad for some money, and then returned to the dorm to get their clothes.

He was gathering their things when a man, stinking of nicotine and body odor, approached him. He had watery, yellow eyes and yellow fingernails.

"What are you doing here by yourself, young man?" the yellow-eyed man asked.

"I'm getting ready to do our laundry," Lonnie said nervously.

The man picked up one of the bags. "Here, I'll help you."

"What are you doing with that boy, Wyman?" another man shouted from a few bunks down. "Is he bothering you, son?"

"Mind your own business, Lucas. This young man's with me." The yellow-eyed man wrapped an arm around Lonnie's shoulders, which made his skin crawl. "You gotta watch out for these guys. Know what I'm saying? But don't you worry. I'll take care of you."

At that moment, a security guard walked in and saw the man with his arm around Lonnie. "Get away from that boy, Wyman," he barked.

"I ain't doing nothing. I'm just trying to help him out, that's all."

"He doesn't need your help," the guard said. "Now get on over to your bunk before I throw you out of here."

The yellow-eyed man quietly slinked back to his bed.

"Are you Lonnie?" the guard asked.

"Yes, sir."

"Your father told me to check on you to see if you were okay."

"I'm all right. I was just getting our dirty clothes together so I could wash them."

"You really shouldn't be up here without your father," the guard said. "It isn't safe. I'm not saying that these men are dangerous, but you can't take any chances. Don't talk to anyone here unless your father's with you." He picked up one of the bags. "I'll help you carry these down."

He escorted Lonnie to the laundry room, which felt much safer than the dorm. Most of the people in there were women with young children.

While their clothes churned in the washer, Lonnie did his homework on a table. The laundry room was noisy, but he couldn't use that as an excuse not to do his work. He had bombed out most of the semester, and he needed to get back on track. If Mr. Treviño was correct when he said that many people became homeless due to bad decisions they'd made in life, Lonnie thought it was time he started making a lot of good ones.

His dad joined him after a while and helped him fold clothes. They took them back to the dorm room and placed them in their locker. The man with the yellow eyes stared at them, but Lonnie didn't say anything to his dad about him. Nothing had happened, and hopefully the man would leave him alone.

They spent their first night at the shelter. Lonnie's dad insisted his son take the top bunk because he felt he would be safer there. Lights went out at ten-thirty. There was some chatting and laughing in the darkness. Eventually, the talking faded, replaced by loud snoring.

Lonnie tossed around restlessly in his bunk, unable to sleep. All night, men got up to use the restroom, and he could see their silhouettes moving in the darkness. If he didn't know better, he could have sworn he saw a pair of watery, yellow eyes, glowing in the dark, staring at him.

He missed his mom. He wanted her to appear to him and say, "What are you doing in this awful place, *mijo*? You don't belong here. Come on, let me take you home."

When he woke up the next morning, he discovered that he had wet the bed. The sheets and his underwear were soaked. He hadn't wet the bed since he was three years old. Feeling humiliated, he climbed off his bunk and woke his dad.

"That's okay, buddy. Don't worry about it. There's nothing to be embarrassed about. We'll just take your sheets to the laundry room, and I'll get you some clean ones. For now, go take a shower."

The last thing Lonnie wanted to do was to shower with a bunch of old, nasty homeless men, but he didn't have a choice.

"Can you go with me?" he asked sheepishly. "I don't want to be in there alone with all those men."

"You bet." His dad had showered the night before, but he stripped off his clothes and joined Lonnie in the shower room. The men laughed and told dirty jokes while they bathed, and Lonnie found the whole experience degrading.

After a quick rinse, he toweled himself off and got dressed. His dad wadded the sheets and told him he would take care of them later. Then they went downstairs for breakfast.

By six o'clock, people headed out of the shelter, like cattle. Lonnie grabbed a push broom and swept the cafeteria floor.

Mr. Marriott stopped by and looked around. He asked Lonnie's dad how their first night had gone.

"Listen, I don't mean to sound ungrateful, but that dorm room ain't no place for a boy Lonnie's age."

"I agree," Mr. Marriott replied. "But it's the only way I can keep you together. The other option is to turn him over to CPS."

"Are you sure there ain't nothing else you can do?" Lonnie's dad asked. "I mean, that room is really scary. Last night, Lonnie . . . " He leaned into Mr. Marriott and whispered in his ear.

Mr. Marriott looked at Lonnie. "I may have something else. Let's go to my office," he said, and they followed him down the hallway.

He shut the door, and after they sat down, he said, "I have a family room available, but like I told you yesterday, those rooms are reserved for women with children. I can let you have it for now, but if a mother and child come in, I may have to ask you to give it up."

"I understand," Lonnie's dad said.

"However, in return, I want you to do something for me."

"Sure, sure. Whatever you want."

"I'd like you to see one of our psychiatrists for counseling."

"A psychiatrist?" Lonnie's dad said indignantly. "I don't need no psychiatrist. I ain't crazy."

"I didn't say you were crazy, Mr. Rodríguez. But the fact is, you've gone through a tremendous amount of stress, with the loss of your wife, your home . . . and now this. I think it would be beneficial for you to speak to one of our mental health providers. I'd also like for you to enroll in our Alcoholics Anonymous program. If you agree to do these things, then I will put you in one of our private family rooms."

Lonnie's dad turned away and stared out the window.

"It's up to you, Mr. Rodríguez."

Grudgingly, he said, "Okay, when can we move into that room?"

"Right now, if you'd like. Let me show you where it is."

The family room had two double beds, a small closet and a chest of drawers. There was a bathroom with a sink, but no shower. Lonnie would continue to bathe at school. But if they were still at the shelter during the Christmas break, he would wash up, using the sink rather than going to the men's shower room upstairs.

They took their bags of clothing out of the dorm and carried them down to their new room.

Afterward, Lonnie was driven to school. Unless he held a cardboard sign that said HOMELESS, there was no reason for anyone to suspect where he had spent the night.

During lunch, Jo Marie approached his table and asked if she could join him. Before eating, she bowed her head and prayed. Out of respect, Lonnie bowed his head, too, and waited quietly.

He wanted to converse with her, but he didn't know what to say. What did churchy girls like to talk about? God? Heaven? The Ten Commandments?

"Have you seen any good movies lately?" he asked, then immediately thought how dumb that line was. He thought she was going to say she had seen a Jesus movie or something.

"We saw *Bride of Frankenstein* on TCM Saturday night," she said.

"Your parents let you watch horror movies?" Lonnie asked, bemused.

"Only the old black and white classics. You know, the ones that starred Boris Karloff, Vincent Price, Lon Chaney . . . those actors."

"That's my real name," Lonnie said.

"What's your real name?"

"Lon Chaney."

Jo Marie laughed. "Get out! Are you serious?"

"Yeah. My full name's Lon Chaney Rodríguez, but everybody calls me Lonnie."

"Why did your parents name you Lon Chaney?"

He explained his name's origin. "So, did you like *Bride of Frankenstein*?"

"Yes, but I've seen it before."

"Have you ever seen *Young Frankenstein*?"

"I don't think so."

"I've got the DVD at home. Listen, I'll let you borrow it if . . . Sorry, I forgot. I don't have it anymore. But rent it sometime. It's worth watching. Believe me, once you see it, you'll never be able to watch that scene in *Bride of*

Frankenstein where the monster meets the blind man, in the same way."

Lonnie didn't remember what else they talked about, but time passed quickly. They didn't share classes, so he wouldn't see her until the following day. Strange, but he looked forward to having lunch with her again.

The first thing Lonnie noticed when he got in the car that afternoon was his dad's short hair and clean-shaven face.

"What do you think, buddy? Is your old man good looking or what?"

"Whoa. Who cut your hair?"

"They got regular barbers that volunteer at the shelter. The counselor I talked with today told me I'd feel better about myself if I got a haircut." Lonnie's dad studied his reflection in the rear-view mirror. "And you know what? I do feel better. If the barbers are still there when we get back, I'll take you to them 'cause you been wolfing out as bad as me."

At the shelter, they underwent the same routine as before: waiting in line, going through the metal detector and signing in. From there, Lonnie's dad took him to their new room.

Lonnie was amazed by how quiet it was, compared to the rest of the building. He would be able to do his homework in there without being distracted by all the noise.

His dad opened the closet, and Lonnie saw their shirts and pants hanging on the wooden rod. Their socks, T-shirts and underwear were folded neatly inside the dresser drawers. As long as he stayed away from the third floor, Lonnie believed he could handle living in the shelter until their situation improved.

"I'm gonna have to put in extra time in the cafeteria today, 'cause I ain't gonna work there tomorrow," his dad said.

"Why not?" Lonnie asked.

"We need money, buddy. So I'm thinking about trying to get one of those catch-out jobs 'cause they pay you the same day you work. But from what I've heard, I gotta get to the catch-out gap early 'cause those jobs go pretty fast. That means I'll have to leave you at the Flournoy Center tomorrow morning."

Lonnie shrugged. "I don't mind. Mr. Marriott said that somebody at the center can take me to school."

After dinner, Lonnie's dad stood behind the serving line and plopped scoops of mashed potatoes and green beans onto plastic trays. If Lonnie still had his cell phone, he would have snapped photos of him feeding the homeless. His mother would have gotten a kick looking at them.

The barbers were gone for the day, so Lonnie wasn't able to get a haircut. But his dad said he would check to see when they would be back.

The next morning, they walked to the Flournoy Center, and after registering Lonnie at the front desk, his dad headed to the catch-out gap.

When Lonnie entered the computer area, he received a shock. Bobby Arbuthnot from his school was sitting in there playing video games.

"What are you doing here?" he asked.

Bobby gawked at him with the same flabbergasted expression. "What are *you* doing here?"

"I didn't know you were homeless," Lonnie said.

"I didn't know *you* were homeless," Bobby said.

"Are you staying at the Helping Hand?"

"Nah, we're at the Shepherd's House."

"How long have you been homeless?"

Bobby sighed. "It's a long story, but it started when our house burned down."

"I remember when that happened," Lonnie said.

"Anyway, me and my mom, my dad and my little brother ended up at the Shepherd's House, and we've been there ever since." He pointed to a group of kids working on puzzles in the next room. "That's my little brother over there."

"How come you never said anything about being homeless?" Lonnie asked.

"Well, it ain't anything anybody brags about. I mean, I'm not ashamed of it or nothing. That's just life. Besides, I know we're not gonna stay like this forever."

"That's how I feel, too," Lonnie said, and he told him about their situation.

He couldn't get over it. Bobby Arbuthnot was homeless. He never would have been able to tell it.

On the way to school, he and Bobby sat together on the Flournoy bus, which looked like any ordinary yellow school bus. It made its first stop at Lamar Elementary, and six kids got off. One little girl looked like she could be a fourth grader, and Lonnie wondered if she was Mr. Treviño's student, Margie.

When they arrived at their school, Lonnie and Bobby got off the bus and made their way to the blacktop like it was nobody's business.

Excitement continued to grow, as teachers and students alike eagerly anticipated the Christmas break. Herman "Slurpee" Gilmore got an early start to his vacation. He was sent home for writing nasty words on a Christmas card and hanging it on a Christmas tree outside the main office. Students had been placing Christmas cards on the tree for Dr. Lambert and the office staff. When Lonnie heard about it, he chuckled to himself. Some things would never change.

At lunchtime, he looked for Jo Marie. She was sitting with her friend, Patricia.

"Can I join you?" Lonnie asked, and sat down without waiting for an answer.

"Pat, did you know that Lonnie's real name is Lon Chaney?" Jo Marie asked.

"So?"

"Don't you know who Lon Chaney was?"

"No."

"Come on, Pat. Lon Chaney was that silent film actor that came out in movies like *Phantom of the Opera* and *The Hunchback of Notre Dame*." Turning to Lonnie, Jo Marie said, "I think you've got the coolest name in the whole school."

"Really? Thanks. Hey, listen, I think I'm going to be able to make it to the Youth Christmas Party after all." With everything Lonnie had gone through, he needed to do something different. Regardless of where they would be staying Sunday night, he was sure his dad could take him to church.

"Awesome!" Jo Marie said. "Now I'll have somebody to dance with."

"Dance? I . . . I don't know how to dance," Lonnie sputtered.

"Don't worry about it, Lon Chaney. I'll teach you how."

After school, as Lonnie was about to climb into the school bus, he spotted his dad parked on the other side of the street.

"See you tomorrow," he told Bobby. Then he caught up to his dad.

"I thought you were working," he said when he stepped in the car.

"I got there too late, and all the jobs were gone," his dad said. "Tomorrow, we'll have to get up extra early, 'cause I need to be at the catch-out gap no later than five-thirty."

"That's okay," Lonnie said. "Don't worry about me. I can stay in our room until the sun comes out. Then I'll walk to the center."

Lonnie volunteered to clean tables in the cafeteria. Since his dad was already working to pay for their stay, he wasn't required to do so, but he felt he owed something to Mr. Marriott for giving them the family room.

The director stopped by, and Lonnie thanked him once again for his generosity.

"I'm glad I had that room available," Mr. Marriott said. "I'm also glad that your father has begun attending the AA meetings."

"You know, my church does a lot of things for the poor," Lonnie said. "Back in July, before school started, they collected shoes to give away to the kids at the Treadwell Orphanage. I was wondering if maybe I should ask our pastor if he wants our church to donate food to the Helping Hand."

"That's a very noble thought, Lonnie," Mr. Marriott said. "We receive plenty of donations from the nearby food banks. But there's a bigger problem that we battle with constantly—a shortage of toiletries—soap, shampoo, toothpaste, toothbrushes, things like that. I hit the hotels in the area all the time for donations, but we never seem to have enough. If you really want your church to help our clients, you might suggest that they put together hygiene kits. All they need to do is get large, plastic baggies and fill them with personal hygiene products. That way, the kits can be handed out individually. Our clients would greatly appreciate them."

"I'll talk to my pastor about it, sir," Lonnie said.

Mr. Marriott picked up a wadded napkin from the floor and tossed it in the trash can. "It's funny how the main thing that comes to people's minds when they see the homeless is that they need food," he said. "But they also need razors and deodorant and soap so they can groom themselves before they go job hunting."

Thinking about his dad, Lonnie realized how true that was.

"Let's go to my office, and I'll type up a list of items our clients need the most so you can present it to your pastor."

Lonnie would definitely score big-time points with Jo Marie if he was to start a hygiene kits drive at church. But more important, he would be doing something—maybe not a lot—but something to help lift someone's spirits.

At lunch, he discussed the hygiene kits idea with Jo Marie. She said she would tell her dad about it, but she also suggested that they bring it up to Mrs. Finley. Perhaps they could start it as their Sunday school project.

CHAPTER TWENTY-SEVEN

FRIDAY WAS THE LAST DAY before the holiday break. Most of the teachers kept their lessons light and assigned what was essentially "busy work" to ride out the time, with the exception of Mr. Arrington.

He wore a wide brim, cowboy hat, a red-plaid shirt, a brown leather vest, denim jeans, leather chaps and cowboy boots. His name for the day was Sheriff Jim. In an exaggerated Texas drawl, he recounted stories of life on the Chisholm Trail and of the dangers cowboys faced driving cattle.

In the middle of his lesson, a commotion broke out in the hallway. At first Lonnie thought kids were fighting, but then he heard Ms. Coronado, the office manager, shout, "Sir! Sir! You can't go in there without signing in at the office first."

"I don't care! I gotta see Lonnie right now!"

Dad?

"Whoa, pardners," Mr. Arrington said. "I'd better see what in tarnation's goin' on out there."

Lonnie's dad burst into the classroom. With tears in his eyes, he cried, "Lonnie! I got a job!"

"Sir, you're going to have to sign in at the office and then get a name badge, or I'm calling security."

Ignoring the office manager, Lonnie's dad said, "The Merriday Trucking Company's hiring me back!"

"Sir! You need to leave our campus right now!" Ms. Coronado demanded, pointing to the door.

"Now hol' on just a cotton-pickin' minute," Mr. Arrington said. "I'm the sheriff in this here town, and I say who stays and who vamooses."

"Mr. Arrington, please!"

"Mr. Arrington? I'm Sheriff Jim, missy," he said, showing Ms. Coronado his five-pointed star badge. He turned to Lonnie's dad. "Tell ya what, pardner. Giddy on down to the office with this little lady and give her yer John Henry. Ya don't wanna end up in the hoosegow, do ya? Then I'll let ya visit a spell with yer little buckaroo."

Lonnie's dad gave him a perplexed look. "I'll be right back," he told Lonnie.

He returned, wearing a name sticker on his shirt. Out in the hallway, he explained what happened.

"I went on a catch-out job this morning, and guess where they sent me? To the Merriday Trucking Company to wash down their trucks. Can you believe it? Of all places. Anyway, as soon as I get there, some of the guys I used to work with see me, and they come over to say hi. At first, I'm kinda embarrassed, you know? I mean, I used to drive those trucks. Now, I'm hosing them down. Pretty soon, my old boss, Mr. Newton, comes out, and he wants to know what I'm doing there, so I tell him. He asks me to go to the office with him. We talk and I explain everything. I also let him know that I've started going to AA. Then I ask him if there's any chance I can get my job back, and . . . " His voice cracked. "He says he can't hire me as a trucker. You know, 'cause of my DWI conviction, but that he can put me on the docks, loading and unloading trucks. 'Course, the job don't pay as good as a trucker's, but it'll still be more than enough money for us to live on."

"Dad, are you serious?" Lonnie said, hardly believing the news.

"Nah, I'm just kidding. Of course I'm serious!"

"So we're moving out of the shelter?"

"Not just yet. The guy I'm replacing is retiring, but he's gonna work till January fifteenth. Then I can have his job. So we'll have to keep living at the shelter till I start getting a regular paycheck. But after that, I'm gonna find us a real nice apartment near here so you won't have to change schools."

He took Lonnie in his arms and held him tightly. Lonnie realized it looked uncool to be seen hugging his dad, but he didn't care. The kids could think whatever they wanted. Anyway, classes were still in session, and the hallways were empty.

"I'm gonna take real good care of you from now on, buddy. Don't you worry. I'm gonna make things right for us."

Lonnie grew teary-eyed. At long last, their own home. Real money coming in. Some stability in their lives. He knew what he wanted to say, but he struggled to get the words out. He couldn't recall ever having uttered them. Finally he looked up and said softly, "I love you, Dad."

"I love you, too, son," his dad replied and kissed him on the forehead.

When Lonnie returned to class, Mr. Arrington asked, "Is everything all right?" There was no trace of the Texas drawl in his voice.

"Yes, sir. Everything . . . everything's going to be fine."

CHAPTER TWENTY-EIGHT

LONNIE INSISTED THAT HIS DAD GO TO CHURCH with him. "God's blessed you with a job, and you need to thank Him for it," he said.

"Yeah, but look at what He put me through to get it."

"Well, you know what they say. God works in mysterious ways."

"Too mysterious, if you ask me. Yeah, sure. I'll go to church with you."

They took their time eating breakfast. The Helping Hand allowed its clients to remain in the shelter all day on the weekends if they wished.

"When we were first married, your mom wanted us to go to church," Lonnie's dad said. "But she was Catholic, and I'd been raised a Baptist. I didn't wanna go to no Catholic church, and she didn't wanna go to a Baptist church, so we wound up not going to church at all."

"I think now would be a good time to start," Lonnie said.

His dad showered upstairs, and Lonnie washed up in their bathroom. His dad returned with his hair neatly combed and his face clean shaven. He wore a blue turtleneck sweater and brown dress slacks.

When they arrived at the church, Brother Pacheco, one of the deacons, greeted them. He tried to steer Lonnie's dad into a Sunday school classroom, but he declined, saying he would wait for his son in the sanctuary. Getting his dad to church was difficult enough. Lonnie wasn't going to push him do anything else.

Jo Marie had spoken to her dad about the hygiene kits project, and he thought it was an excellent idea. He said he would present it to the congregation during the service. Mrs. Finley was also aware of it, but she let Lonnie make the announcement to the class.

"As everybody knows, Marsville's got a huge homeless problem," Lonnie told the group.

"I know, man," Nathan Fambro said. "They're like cockroaches. They're everywhere."

Lonnie scowled at him. "Don't call them that. They're regular people, just like me and you. Except that they're going through a real hard time. Believe it or not, what happened to them could just as easily happen to any of us. To you, to you, to you," he said, pointing around the room, "and to me. I know I'm not smart enough to fix the homeless problem. I don't even know if it *can* be fixed. But I know one thing we can do. We can collect toiletries for them."

"Toiletries?" Nathan snickered. "Like what? Toilet paper?"

"Quiet, Nathan," Jo Marie scolded him.

"One of the reasons some homeless people can't find jobs is 'cause they're real grungy-looking," Lonnie continued, ignoring Nathan's stupid comment. "But if we were to give them things like combs and razors, bars of soap, toothpaste and toothbrushes, then maybe they could make themselves look nicer when they go out to look for jobs. So what I want is for our class to start collecting toiletries for the homeless. And when we have enough, we'll put them in baggies. Then I want our class to take them to the Helping Hand, a homeless shelter downtown, to pass them out."

A lot of heads nodded in agreement.

"Jo Marie's dad is going to ask the church to help with the project, but I want our class to be in charge of it."

"Is there a particular reason why you've chosen the Helping Hand for us to work with?" Mrs. Finley asked.

"Um . . . well, Mr. Marriott, the director, is a friend of ours, and me and my dad are pretty familiar with the place," Lonnie told her without elaborating.

After class, Jo Marie approached him. "I've never seen this side of you, Lon Chaney. I feel like I'm only now getting to know you."

"Same here," he said. "I guess there's a lot we don't know about each other."

Before the start of the service, Lonnie invited his dad to sit with him and the youth in front.

Brother Beasley opened with "O Come, All Ye Faithful." While Lonnie's dad sang, some of the kids stared at him, amazed by his deep, clear voice.

"He sings in a band," Lonnie whispered to Jo Marie.

After church, Brother Beasley praised Lonnie's dad for his singing talent. "I could hear you above everyone else. Have you ever thought about joining our choir?"

"I ain't a member here," he said.

"Well, if you're searching for a church home, perhaps you might want to consider this one."

"We'll see."

Lonnie and his dad had lunch at the Golden Corral, an all-you-can-eat buffet restaurant. It was the fanciest place at which they had eaten in a long time. With money in his pocket from his catch-out jobs, Lonnie's dad said he felt like splurging. There were dozens of food choices at the buffet line, plus desserts, and they ate like kings.

"Your grandparents Salinas called," Lonnie's dad said. "They want us to spend Christmas with them."

"Can we?" Lonnie asked, knowing how his dad felt about them.

"Sure, why not? They're still your grandparents. I don't wanna keep you from seeing them. Just don't say nothing about us being homeless."

"We're not homeless," Lonnie said. "We have a home. And pretty soon, we're going to get another one."

"A much better one, buddy. A much, much better one."

Lonnie finished his peach cobbler, then pushed his plate away. Sitting back in his chair, he asked, "In the movie *The Ring*, how many days did the characters have to live after they watched a certain video?"

"I don't know. Thirteen?"

"Come on, Dad. We watched it back in the summer. It was seven."

"Well, I think thirteen's a better number. You know, 'cause thirteen's bad luck. And speaking of thirteen, do you remember how the audiences in the movie theaters were able to see the ghosts in the original movie, *13 Ghosts*?"

"Didn't you tell me they had to wear special Ghost Viewers?"

"Hey, buddy. You got a sharp memory."

Lonnie's dad looked happy and relaxed. As far as Lonnie could tell, he hadn't had a beer all week. Soon, he would start working at the Merriday Trucking Company again, which Lonnie saw as a belated Christmas present for the both of them.

With school out, Lonnie would have to spend his days at the Flournoy Center, but at least Bobby Arbuthnot would be there to keep him company. Or maybe not. Hopefully, Bobby and his family would be living in a house or in an apartment before long.

That evening, Lonnie returned to church for the Youth Christmas Party. He encouraged his dad to stay for it, worried that if he didn't have anything to do, he might be tempted to go out and drink.

A large barrel had been set up in the atrium, with a sign taped to it that said: TOILETRIES. A few items had already been dropped in it. Mr. Marriott had recommended that donors buy travel-size products to make it more convenient for his clients to carry them. Brother Elrod stressed that when he made the announcement about the project.

The fellowship hall was decorated with streamers and Christmas lights. There were tables with sandwiches, cookies, chips and punch. Oldies rock music mixed with Christmas songs played in the background.

Ms. Reese, the youth director, tried to get the kids to dance, but except for a few daring souls, almost everyone shied away.

"Why don't you ask one of those little girls to dance with you, buddy?" Lonnie's dad asked.

"No, Dad. I don't know how to dance."

"Come on, Mr. Rodríguez," Ms. Reese said, taking him by the hand. "Let's show them how it's done."

"Wait, I . . . I ain't danced in years."

"Go on, Dad," Lonnie said, laughing. "Show us how."

His dad followed Ms. Reese to the center of the room. Lonnie expected him to look foolish, but his dad impressed him with his moves. As big as he was, he glided across the floor with grace and ease. Pretty soon, other adults and kids joined them.

"Dance with me, Lon Chaney," Jo Marie told him.

"I don't know how to dance," he said.

"No one does until they start. Come on, I'll teach you."

Why not? Lonnie thought. If his dad was willing to give it a try, so would he. With so many people dancing, no one would notice if he messed up. At first, he tried to imitate Jo Marie, but as he got into the rhythm of the music, he improvised his moves.

He looked over at his dad and Ms. Reese. It was weird seeing him with another woman. But Lonnie realized that eventually, his dad would marry again. Not anytime soon, he hoped, though he knew his dad was too young to spend the rest of his life alone.

"Let's go see if anyone's brought more toiletries," he told Jo Marie when the dance number ended. They walked to the atrium and looked inside the barrel. A few more items had been added.

"This is a really good idea," Jo Marie said. "Thank you for organizing it." She reached up and hugged Lonnie. As he held her in his arms, he felt a strong desire to kiss her. He thought she would have let him, but he resisted the urge and pulled away. It was too early. Maybe later, but the moment didn't feel right.

After the party, Lonnie and his dad drove back to the shelter.

"Did you have a good time, buddy?"

"Yeah, I did. How about you?"

"Pretty good. The people there sure are nice." He paused, then said, "I wonder what my family would think if I became a Presbyterian."

CHAPTER TWENTY-NINE

"MERRY CHRISTMAS!"

Lonnie's dad and his in-laws embraced each other warmly, apparently willing to forget the past. Uncle Beto and Uncle Rubén, their wives and Lonnie's cousins, Socorro and Amanda, were there, too.

"What do you want me to do with the presents?" Lonnie asked his grandpa.

"Put them under the Christmas tree."

Candles were lit throughout the house, emitting a scent of apple and cinnamon. Green garlands with red bows were draped across each entryway. Kindling crackled in the fireplace and Christmas music wafted from the stereo. Lonnie was glad to be at his grandparents' house, but his heart ached, knowing this would be their first Christmas without his mom.

For dinner, they ate tamales, rice and beans. Dessert included buñuelos and cinnamon tea.

Lonnie's grandpa asked his son-in-law how they were doing, and he told everyone they were doing great. He said he was back at the Merriday Trucking Company, and they were now living at the Willow Tree Apartments near Lonnie's school. Those things wouldn't be true for a while, but no one needed to know that.

"And Lonnie's got this project going where he's gonna get people at his church to donate toiletries, like soap and deodorant and toothpaste. Then he and the kids in his Sunday school class are gonna hand them out to the homeless people at a shelter downtown. Lonnie came up with that idea all by himself."

"How wonderful," Lonnie's grandma said. "I don't know of any other thirteen-year-old who would think of doing something like that. These days, most kids only think about themselves. Forget about helping others."

"Your mami would be so proud of you, *mijo*," his grandpa said.

"Speaking of Becky," Uncle Beto said, "Rubén and I ordered a headstone for her grave. It'll be ready the week after New Year's Day, and I'd like for all of us to go to the cemetery to see it and to say a few words."

They opened Christmas presents. Lonnie's grandparents gave him a winter jacket, for which he was grateful, because his old one barely fit, and they didn't have the money to buy another one. Uncle Rubén gave him a watch. Lonnie didn't own a watch and never felt he needed one because he had always relied on his cell phone to keep track of the time. But until his dad could afford to get him a new phone, the watch would come in handy. His grandma frowned when he opened Uncle Beto's present.

"Ay, Beto, why are you giving Lonnie that junk?"

"This isn't junk, Grandma," Lonnie said, holding up a DVD of *Brain Eaters from the Black Hills*.

"I know you like horror movies, so I thought you'd enjoy that one," Uncle Beto said.

"Let me give you my presents," Lonnie's dad said and passed them out.

His mother-in-law tore open the wrapping from the box and took out a porcelain figurine of a little girl with her arms around her mother's waist.

"That's a Lladró," Lonnie's dad explained. "Becky liked to collect them, but me and Lonnie don't need those fancy things, so I thought you'd like to have it."

His mother-in-law's eyes teared up. "This is so beautiful," she said and kissed him on the cheek.

Uncle Beto and his family received a Lladró Don Quixote figurine and Uncle Rubén and his family, one of a ballerina.

Lonnie's dad was given gift cards: to Red Lobster, Macy's and Home Depot.

After they left, Lonnie wasn't ready to return to the shelter, so he asked his dad if he could drive them through the R Streets to look at Christmas lights. His dad agreed, but said that it would have to be a short trip because he had to conserve the gas in his car.

As they drove, Lonnie wondered what it would be like to live in one of those mansions, to live in that kind of luxury. He also wondered if the people who lived in those houses had any idea that there were thousands of men, women and children who would be spending Christmas night without a decent place to sleep.

"You know what?" his dad said after a while. "I'm thinking about us going to Abilene for New Year's Day."

Lonnie sat up. "Seriously?"

"Yeah. My parents always throw a big New Year's Day party, and I figure that if I'm gonna see your mom's family, I oughta see mine, too." He grew quiet for a moment. "You know, I've made a lotta mistakes, and I'll probably keep making them. But that ain't no reason to stay away from my family. Besides, they're your family, too, and I ain't got no right to keep you from them."

Lonnie thought it would be great to see Rita, Henry K and Julián again. He would've liked to have moved to

Abilene, but after spending the past few weeks in hell, he was thankful for the chance to live in a real home again.

"Hey, buddy. I'm getting kinda tired of listening to Christmas music. Find another radio station, would you?"

"It's Christmas, Dad. I think they're all playing Christmas songs."

"Then pop in a CD or something."

Lonnie opened the console and took out a Los Brujos demo CD, one of several his dad kept in his car. The first song was titled "Caught in a Moment of Time."

"You know, I never did hear back from the owner of the Club Monte Carlo," Lonnie's dad said. "I guess he's decided to stick with DJs. That's all right. When I start working, I won't need to be out at night, trying to make extra money."

"So does this mean that Los Brujos is breaking up again?" Lonnie asked.

"Yeah, I think so. I'm getting kinda old to be playing in a band." His dad turned down the volume. "Listen, buddy, I'm real sorry I didn't have money to buy you Christmas presents this year. But as soon as we get our things out of storage, I want you to have my guitar. That'll be my present to you. I'll teach you how to play it real good. I want you to practice every night, and then . . . " He paused. "Well, maybe on the weekends or when you ain't got homework. I want you to do real good in school, so you can go to college, maybe to Hardin-Simmons or SMU. And then one day, you'll make a lotta money and have a house out here on the Rich Streets."

"Maybe," Lonnie said. "But right now, I'll settle for having a place to live in other than the shelter."

At the Helping Hand, Lonnie sat on his bed and studied the DVD cover of *Brain Eaters from the Black Hills*. According to the synopsis, the movie was about zombies that attack an army fort in the 1800's. A movie about Union soldiers fighting zombies. How cool was that? Of course, he wouldn't be able to watch it, until they moved out of the shelter, and they took their TV and DVD player out of storage.

It didn't matter. He knew how the movie would end. The zombies would eventually kill all the soldiers or turn them into zombies. Still, he looked forward to sitting down in their own apartment to watch it.

Their own apartment. He could hardly wait.

EPILOGUE

LONNIE DIDN'T KNOW IF HE WOULD EVER FULLY understand why his mother had to die so young. The Bible tracts Jo Marie gave him didn't provide the answers he was looking for. Maybe there were no answers. Or maybe the answers were so complicated, they went beyond his ability to comprehend. In any case, he had given up trying to figure it out, except to say that it happened, and he had to move on. Otherwise, the not knowing would drive him crazy.

Every day, though, he felt his mother's presence in his life. After they moved into their apartment, and he began arranging the furniture, he kept thinking: *This is where Mom would've put the sofa and the television. This is where she would've sat the china cabinet. This is where she would've hung these pictures.*

Lonnie's dad continued to return to the shelter for his AA meetings. Lonnie would have been okay with it if his dad had an occasional beer, but as far as he could tell, his dad had given up drinking completely.

"I messed things up once, and I ain't planning on doing it again," he told Lonnie.

His dad showered and shaved every day, even though his job didn't require him to be neatly groomed. He had also lost a few pounds and looked healthier than he had in years.

There was a rap on Lonnie's bedroom door. "Hey, buddy. You up?"

"Yeah, I'm just about ready."

"The preacher said he wants us at the church by eight."

"I know. I'll be out in a minute."

Lonnie finished making his bed. He picked up his watch, cell phone and wallet from his desk. As he did, he looked down at his book report sitting on top. He had gotten an A on it. The book, a horror story titled *Mrs. Leigon's Grave*, was one of the most enjoyable books he had read in a long time. A few more A's in Progressive Reading and maybe next year, he could be placed in an advance reading class with Axel.

Lonnie decided he would never be great at math or science. But the B's and occasional C's he had been making in those classes weren't too bad, either.

He pulled back his curtain and looked out. Frost had formed outside his window. Thirty-six degrees was predicted to be the high for the day, but he would guess the current temperature was no more than twenty-five. Perfect weather for sleeping in, but he couldn't do that. They had things to do.

The night before, Lonnie and the kids in his Sunday school class had bagged up three hundred fifty-seven hygiene kits. Brother Elrod told them to meet at church the next morning before they headed out to the Helping Hand to distribute them.

"I fixed you some chorizo and egg taquitos," Lonnie's dad said when Lonnie walked into the kitchen. "It's gonna be a long day, so I want you to eat before we leave."

"Thanks, Dad."

"You might need to heat them up," he said.

Lonnie bit into one. "They're fine." He took the orange juice carton from the fridge and poured himself a glass. Then he joined his dad at the table.

"I guess it's gonna feel kinda weird for you to go back to the shelter, huh?" his dad said.

"Yeah, but maybe a lot of the people who were there with us will be gone. What I mean is, hopefully they found jobs and a better place to live."

"I wish that was true, buddy," his dad said. "But the fact is, we were lucky, plain and simple. Some of those people who stay there, they've given up. I see them when I go to my meetings. They don't think about things getting better. They're like zombies, going nowhere."

"I know that giving homeless people a little bag of toiletries isn't a whole lot," Lonnie said. "But at least we can show them that somebody cares about them."

"I wish your mom could see you right now," his dad said. "She'd be so proud of the man you're turning out to be. I know I am."

"I think she'd be proud of the both of us," Lonnie said.

After breakfast, they drove to the church. Jo Marie and her parents had already arrived. So had Mr. and Mrs. Finley, Ms. Reese and a number of other kids and their parents. They loaded up the church van with boxes of hygiene kits. Before leaving, Brother Elrod explained the importance of their mission. He said they were going to the shelter to help and not to be critical of the people they saw.

"As it says in Matthew, chapter seven, 'Do not judge, or you too will be judged. For in the same way you judge others, you will be judged, and with the measure you use, it will be measured to you."

"Amen," Lonnie's dad said.

From there, they headed to the Helping Hand. Lonnie and his dad rode in the van because they needed to guide Mr. Bullock, the driver, where to park once they arrived.

Some of the kids grew nervous when they saw the large groups of men lounging outside the shelter.

Nathan Fambro turned to Lonnie and said, "Man, this place sucks."

"I know. Trust me, Nathan, I know. But like Brother Elrod said, we're not here to judge."

Mr. Marriott met them at the entrance. Lonnie was happy to see that Mr. Treviño and his wife were with him. They all gathered in the cafeteria, where Mr. Marriott went over the procedure for distributing the kits. The boxes were placed on the top of six long tables, and helpers were assigned to each section. Brother Elrod led the group in a prayer, and then the clients were called in.

In assembly-line fashion, Lonnie and the other volunteers handed out the kits. Having spent time at the shelter, Lonnie knew some of the people there could be rough and unruly, but everyone accepted their gift graciously and offered a humble "thank you" and "God bless you."

Altogether, three hundred, thirty-five bags were given out. Mr. Marriott told the group that he would keep the rest of the kits in his office for clients who might need them later. When they were through, he called everyone together to express his appreciation for their work.

"And I especially want to thank Lonnie Rodríguez for initiating this wonderful project," he said. "If it wasn't for him, our clients wouldn't have received this special blessing today."

Everyone applauded, and Lonnie beamed with pride.

Mrs. Finley, who had been taking pictures, asked him to pose with Mr. Marriott. Lonnie then invited his dad and Mr. Treviño to join them for another photo.

He hoped his mother was looking down at him from heaven. If she was, he would like to believe that she'd be pointing at him and shouting to the angels, "Look everybody! That's my son!"

Also by Ray Villareal

Alamo Wars

Body Slammed!

Don't Call Me Hero

My Father, the Angel of Death

Who's Buried in the Garden?